DERANGED DEMONS

DERANGED DEMONS

GAME OF PSYCHOS
BOOK ONE

MIA HARTSON

ISBN: 978-0-6457298-4-9
First printing edition 2024 in United States
Cover design by Trif Book Design

Mia Hartson
PO BOX 1052, Golden Grove Village, SA 5125
www.miahartson.com

Let me in, princess...
~ Dante

~

Because everyone deserves love, even the broken ones...

~

Please note: This is a reverse harem romance, meaning our sassy leading female will end up happily mated to multiple males by the end of the series.
While this is mostly a light-hearted read, please be aware that this series includes mature language, torture, mention of traumatic childhood pasts, and violence. Please take care of yourself when reading this story. xx

CHAPTER

ONE

~ Princess Blake ~

I fold my arms across my chest and stare at the male prisoner slumped on a metal chair. Trey, his name is, according to my intel. He's positioned in the middle of the dank cell, his fine black suit torn with blood smeared on his sleeve cuffs. A distinct tattoo of a blade is visible on his collarbone, the black ink half obscured by his shirt, but still easily identifying him as a member of the Fallon Blade clan. *Since when are the demons of the Fallon Blade clan traitors? I know they have a knack for causing trouble in the city, but I didn't expect them to side with the witches. Then again, I didn't think any demon would be dumb enough to ally with those genocidal maniacs, and yet,*

Trey isn't the first traitor we've caught in recent months. *Something seriously fucked up is going on here.*

"Again," I instruct the burly demon guard hovering before Trey. Without hesitation, Hansen smashes his fist into Trey's jaw. Blood sprays, and Trey's head whips to the side at the impact. One of the traitor's golden teeth flies from his mouth, falling to the floor and almost disappearing down the small grate situated beneath his black cap toe boots.

There's a moment of silence as Trey stares at his tooth like he can't believe what he's looking at, and then he meets my gaze with hate-filled eyes. *Huh. Who knew his teeth would be his weakness?* He glares at me like I've just killed his lover rather than dislodged a tooth, but then he schools his expression, and his mouth stretches into a crazed smile. *Ah, there it is.* All demons show their inner psycho eventually. Even the ones who like to pretend otherwise. It's in our nature.

Even mine. Though, unlike Trey, I make it a point to own my craziness. Being the daughter of the most feared demon king in history comes with expectations. *High* expectations. I wouldn't even be here if I hadn't learned to claw my way up and prove to the demons that I'm more than the half-angel trash they'd believed I was when my mother had dumped me on the palace doorstep. They hadn't accepted my mother either, which is why I suspect she'd never taken her place as queen. Well, that and the fact that she'd disappeared soon after the king had proposed to her.

In any case, I'm pretty sure Trey is actually a half-decent guy, and the thought of torturing him is leaving a sour taste in my mouth. It doesn't help that I was called from my bed in the middle of the day for this. Dad usually handles these situations, but on this occasion, I'd had to step up. In fact, I've had to step up a lot lately, taking over increasingly more of the king's duties, and it's starting to make me worry.

"Is this all you've got, princess?" Trey goads, spitting blood onto the floor. "I've been in street brawls worse than this."

"*Now that's probably the only truthful thing he's said so far,*" Shade's sarcastic comment sounds in my mind. Perched on my shoulder, the crow's clawed feet grip the leather shoulder pad I had designed just for her. "*What's your angle here, Blake?*" she continues. Her beady black eyes lock onto Trey as she speaks in my head, the pair of us having a silent conversation. No one knows Shade and I can speak to each other like this. Sure, they're aware I can control the crows and use them to spy in the city or attack when needed, but not that I can have full conversations with the birds in my mind. Although, half the time I forget to think my response and end up saying the words out loud instead. Which is probably why the demons think I'm crazy.

"*You've been at this for a while, and this cell smells like something died in a giant's asshole,*" Shade complains. "*I'm pretty sure our new friend couldn't tell you anything useful even if he wanted to. He's too oblivious to be the head of this operation.*"

I'm tempted to ask whether she actually knows what a giant's ass smells like, but I only nod my head at Hansen. The guard hits Trey in the face again, and this time, I hear a crack. For a moment, I think Hansen has broken Trey's neck, but then the demon lifts his head and starts to laugh hysterically.

"What's the bet he's about to say something stupid?" Shade chimes in again.

I ignore her, but only because I'm too busy thinking about the king's most decorated general who's shifting impatiently behind me. If I don't get something out of Trey soon, General Josek will take matters into his own hands, and that would not be pretty. General Josek isn't just crazy, he's downright unhinged, which is probably why he's my father's favorite. No doubt, the traitorous demon in the chair before me doesn't realize I'm the only one standing between him and unimaginable torture. General Josek had wanted to start this interrogation with much more creative methods, and I'm the one who talked him down. Partly because I enjoy irritating the fuck out of the general, and partly because despite his strange attachment to his teeth and the damning evidence against him, Trey seems reasonably harmless. He's also young, only eighteen, which is practically a baby in demon years, and he likely just got caught up in the plans of his clan. His *gift,* the unique power that all demons get as they mature, is also one of the least useful ones I've heard of. The male has the power to change his hair color at will, and while that might be handy when it's time to hit the nightclubs, it's not going to help him now.

Besides, usually when faced with the idea of excruciating pain, demons will just blab anything to save themselves. You probably wouldn't know the truth from the lies. At that thought, my mind wanders to the she-demon I encountered not too long ago. *Scarlett.* She'd obviously been through a lot by the time I'd found her using her power to extract the truth from her disloyal brother. The ability to use magic to determine the truth is a rare gift that I could use in this very situation, and I'm likely going to have to get her help sometime soon.

"You have to know this is going to end badly for you unless you tell us what the witches are planning," I say to Trey. "And why we found you with a crate of illegal explosives that are clearly of witch origin. Give us something useful, and you might just survive this."

Trey sneers, though I see a flicker of fear in his coal-black eyes. "Even if I knew their plans, I wouldn't tell you, you half-angel bitch. For all we know, you're not even a true heir to the throne. Your mother probably dumped you here knowin' you'd get a free ride. No, the demons deserve whatever the witches bring down on them." He laughs again like he thinks he's accomplished some great feat by saying that to me, but all it's done is ensure his death. *Oh, Trey.* I sigh inwardly.

I sense General Josek starting to move behind me, probably readying himself to cut out Trey's tongue for his blatant disrespect. It's one thing to curse me, but another thing entirely to question my legitimacy to the throne. The seasoned general might hate me, but he swore an oath to protect me and my father, and he won't let this slide. I unsheathe my blades, knowing I should get to Trey first. If I hesitate, General Josek and Hansen will see it as weakness.

Neither of us make it to Trey before the demon shouts another slur at me, and he grinds his jaw with force, detaching another one of his golden teeth. There's a wild look in his eyes as he chews, and his vibrant yellow hair seems to drain of color, changing to a pure white. Within a matter of seconds, green froth starts bubbling from his mouth. *Well, shit.*

"Huh. I guess they weren't just teeth after all," I send to Shade.

"It's some kind of pill!" Hansen shouts, gripping Trey's jaw like he intends to remove the tooth, but before he can shove his fingers into the demon's throat, Trey's body turns to ash and the only sound is the clatter of his horns hitting the stone floor. The long-curved horns are the only part of Trey that's left. Well, that and his clothes which crumple to the ground.

"Now that I did not expect," Shade comments.

I frown at the empty chair. *"You and me both."*

Clearing my throat, I wipe the look of shock from my face. "That wasn't just a suicide pill," I say aloud, feeling the gravity of what we've just witnessed. "That was another weapon."

General Josek steps up beside me, and his voice is a harsh rasp in my ear. "We need to alert the king."

I don't acknowledge him as I move to collect Trey's horns. They're still warm and the feel of the knobbly ridges against my fingers makes my stomach churn. It's weird to think that Trey's gone, but his power, the power that's stored in his horns, is now in my hands.

As I go to stride from the room, General Josek calls out, "Princess Blake." It's the first time he's said my name in a long while, and it sends a prickle of unease down my spine.

"The prisoner didn't know anything," I say bluntly as my only explanation of what happened. Twisting my head, I peer back, taking in the severe expression on his face. "Make sure this gets cleaned up, then take Hansen and as many as you need to the Fallon Blade clan house. See if you can get anyone else to talk. He wasn't working alone." I know I should consult with the king before giving the order, but this is too important, and if Dad is intent on letting me handle this, I'm going to show that I have my shit together.

"Yes, your highness," General Josek replies, his thin lips curving upwards at the sides, and his dark eyes flashing with satisfaction.

Great. I've just let him loose on the Fallon Blade clan, I mutter internally to Shade.

While normally I would sympathize, I think it's safe to say they deserve it, she replies, and I know she's right. Because the clan should have known better than to work with the witches. Even a demon as young as Trey.

The power inside the traitor's horns makes my hands tingle, urging me to move, and I exit the cell, unable to shake the sense of foreboding working through me. *This is much worse than I thought.*

The royal palace is more of a giant fortress than a place of grandeur, with thick reinforced stone walls, six-inch steel doors that lock at the end of each corridor, hidden rooms that house extra food stores and supplies, and finely crafted weapons as the main form of decoration along the walls.

I'm told it wasn't always like this. According to the scholars in the palace library, there was a time when everything was lavish and tasteful, the large building designed more with the idea of pleasure and seduction in mind. But that was before the war with the witches and the great battle, during which half of the palace was destroyed. When the structure was rebuilt, the king still had the battle at the forefront of his mind, and designs were made to ensure we'd be more prepared if it ever happened again.

Truthfully, I used to think the king had overdone it, especially because as far as we all knew, the witches had been wiped out completely. But now, with the multiple incidents in the city, and evidence that some of the witches still live, I'm starting to think Dad really is the smartest demon in Seral. *Guess you have to be when you're the ruler of this place.*

At that thought, my brows lower. Thankfully, demons are immortal, so becoming queen isn't something I have to worry about for the most part, but there are ways a demon can die, not to mention Dad might one day want to retire. I cringe as I push that thought to the back of my mind.

"So, are we going to talk about what just happened?" Shade asks as we round another corner. Thankfully, she doesn't hear all my thoughts, but only what I send when I'm using my magic to converse with her.

"General Josek will extract information from the Fallon Blade demons," I reply as I make my way past a row of axes that look large enough to sever a giant's head. I turn down another corridor before stopping in front of a tall black statue of a gargoyle. Twisting my head from side-to-side, I make sure we're not being watched, then I touch the left clawed pinkie toe of the monster. The statue is made from polished black marble, but at my touch, the stone warms beneath my fingertip and a secret door opens in the wall behind the sculpture. Shade and I slip into the dark tunnel, and the door closes behind us, sealing us in. Blinking, I let my eyes adjust to the darkness, the pitch black changing to a lighter shade of gray, and I begin making my way along the narrow tunnel and down a curving flight of stone steps.

"Until he returns, there's not much we can do," I say to Shade, continuing our conversation. I could, of course,

meet the general at the Fallon Blade clan house, but I'm not in the mood to see him at work.

I make my way down the last steps, then move onto a landing. A thick steel door marked with silver whirls and patterns blocks our path ahead, and I stride over. When I'm directly in front of it, a small panel on the door opens and light streams out, scanning my retina. It's technology a designer loyal to my father picked up in the human realm, and there's the tell-tale tone identifying me as an approved individual before a click sounds. I whisper the words that only the king and I know, and the door shudders before sliding to the side, revealing the room beyond.

Lights flare to life like tiny suns dotting the ceiling high above, and invisible streams of power rush at me, reaching out through the open door. Sucking in a breath, I try to ignore the feeling as I walk forward, moving between the high walls packed with rows upon rows of glass cabinets, each housing a different set of demon horns. Shade makes a clicking sound as the door closes shut behind us, but I keep my attention on the path ahead. Power swirls in the air, trapped in the vault, and there's a strange metallic taste on my tongue.

The glass cabinets keep most of the power encased, but remnants leak out, and with this many pairs of horns, that power builds. I'm surprised none of the servants or guards in the palace have felt it yet. Even if the vault is so far underground.

They're not just horns, I remind myself. *They're*

evidence of lives lived. Of the demons who once walked the land of Seral. The vault is a tomb of sorts. Low and high born alike, the horns of the dead are all here. *Even the horns of a traitor,* I think as I flap my black feathery wings, lifting into the air until I find one of the empty cabinets on a higher shelf. Carefully, I deposit Trey's horns and shut the small glass door, glad to have them out of my hands.

"You know, if the witches ever find this place and get their hands on all this power..." Shade begins, but I'm quick to stop her train of thought.

"They won't," I respond aloud, letting out a deep breath. Then I amend, "They can't." In the wrong hands, these horns, this *power,* could be a weapon, and one that couldn't be allowed to fall to the witches.

Back before the ordeal with the witches, a demon was buried, horns and all. A demon's power remained in their horns, even after life, but we were unable to harness this power, so instead we buried the dead. The power would leak into the ground like tree roots, giving life to the land until that power naturally depleted. But then the witches figured out how to steal the power for themselves. They started robbing our graves and taking the horns of the recently deceased. By the time the king realized what was happening, nearly all of the grave sites had been defiled, and the witches were enjoying their new gifts.

Everything escalated until the witches started murdering demons to obtain more power. They were willing to destroy demonkind, and it was only because

King Dalton managed to convince the other five realms to ally and join the fight against the witches that the demons survived. I was born centuries after that, but I've heard all the harrowing tales.

Now when a demon dies, it's law that their horns are to be delivered to the king. And with the horns in these sealed cabinets, the power never goes back into the earth. It never depletes.

I stare across the vault, at the varying shapes and colors of horns, a twinge of envy pinching in my gut. Reaching up, I brush my hand over my head and comb my fingers through my raven-colored hair. I wouldn't have to worry about making an addition to this tomb. I was born without horns or a tail, and I don't even know where my power comes from. It's different for angels, the king has told me, and we both assume that when it comes to this, I'm a little more like my mother.

Shade pecks my neck lightly as I flap my wings, slowly dropping to the ground, and I scrunch my face at the ticklish sensation.

"Hey, cut it out," I laugh.

"*Not until you stop feeling sorry for yourself,*" Shade replies, pecking me a few more times. "*Don't tell me you're thinking about what that scum traitor said about you.*"

"What? No," I reply, but now that she's mentioned it, I replay Trey's words in my head. No one has had the guts to speak to me like that for a long time, and hearing it was a reminder that no matter what I do, I'll never be enough for the demons. No matter what I do, I'll always be different, and in their eyes, that means I'm not fit to be a royal.

"Well, he's not entirely wrong," I say, feigning indifference. "I *am* a half-angel." I sometimes wish that the king would have found a demon mate rather than my mother, but it's not like we get to choose our fated mates. I just try to remind myself that Lady Fate must have her reasons for matching those two, even if I can't see it yet.

Demons don't believe in the gods and goddesses that are worshipped in some of the other realms, but many do believe in destiny and the idea that our fates are determined by an actual female entity we name 'Lady Fate.' I figure she must be real, because someone has to be responsible for the matchmaking mess that sometimes goes on.

"Hmm, yes he has a point, and sometimes you are a bit of a bitch," Shade teases.

I'm about to swat her from my shoulder when a rush of power slides down my back, thick invisible fingers brushing along my skin and making me shiver. I spin, turning to the small black door situated at the other end of the vault. There's another retina scanner, but this one would incinerate me if I moved within range. It's the only place in the entire palace that only the king has access.

"What do you think is in there?" I say to Shade curiously. We've debated the question many times over the years.

"I'm still sticking with my answer. A sex room," she answers bluntly.

I snort a laugh. *"We both know the king isn't shy about his many fetishes."* In fact, I wouldn't mind if he did become a bit more secretive in that department. Demons as a general rule, are very open, but when it comes to family there are some things a daughter doesn't need to see.

My thoughts sober as more power radiates down my spine. *"Well, whatever is in there, it's something incredibly powerful."*

Shade ruffles her feathers like she can feel it, too. *"And by that, you mean something dangerous."*

"Precisely."

Unease goes through me as I turn my back on the door and begin striding toward the exit. I've only made it two steps when I swear I feel a fingertip brush along the shell of my right ear. I hear the faintest whisper, the voice reminding me of the crashing waves of the ocean, but the words aren't loud enough for me to make out.

"Did you hear that?" I ask, speaking aloud as my eyes flare wide. I spin back around, and a glimmer of light outlines the frame of the door. It's gone again an instant later, and I'm not sure if I imagined it.

"Hear what?" Shade replies as I continue to stare.

I blink but the glowing light doesn't reappear, and I don't hear the voice again. *Sooo I'm hearing other voices now? Great.* I hope it's something to do with my power, like how I can speak to Shade, but something tells me it isn't. All I know for sure is that whatever is behind that door, I probably don't want to find out.

I remain there until Shade questions me again, then I mumble that it was nothing and leave the vault. But even as I climb the steps, I can't stop thinking about what's behind the black door, and what the king has been hiding all these years.

CHAPTER

TWO

~ Princess Blake ~

I stride over the glossy black tiles and make my way up the long corridors of the palace. When I reach the third floor, two broad armored guards are standing sentry outside the king's private chambers. The guards are both attractive, even if they have pinched expressions like they've just tasted something foul. Though, I guess their stern attitude is to be expected considering they work for my father. As I approach, I take in the corded muscles on their thick arms which are easily wider than my head, and my brows rise.

"Looks like Dad upgraded his security," I send to Shade.

"I'll say," she replies appreciatively. *"Check out the muscular thighs on that one."*

I have to cough to stop my laughter, but my gaze slides lower on the guard standing to the right. She isn't wrong. The male is a beast, with rippling muscles all over. *"Looks like someone doesn't skip leg day,"* I muse back, and there's a cawing sound in my head that I know is her laughter.

Sometimes I wonder how I got so lucky finding Shade. I'd been in the human realm chasing down a demon when I'd entered a human dwelling and came across her cage. I'd thought she was dead, her feathered body a motionless bundle in a pile of birdseed, but when I'd reached out with my power, she'd begun speaking in my mind, pleading for help. I'd been startled as it was the first time my gift had presented, and it took me a good moment before I realized what was happening. When I came to my senses, I knew I had to do something. It's against the rules to tamper with the human realm beyond what is necessary, but I brought her back to Seral and nursed her to health anyway. We have crows here, so it wasn't hard to hide her origin from the king. Still, I keep dreading the day she'll ask to return to the human realm.

"If you keep staring like that, he's going to get the wrong idea," Shade points out, jolting me from my thoughts, and I realize I'm still staring at the guard.

"Or the right one," I send back, but my gaze snaps up, and I mentally remind myself of Trey, the witches,

and why I'm here. Not slowing my stride, I move closer to the guards. "Stand aside, muscles, I have an urgent matter to discuss with the king," I order. I expect them to open the double doors just as I reach them, but instead, they cross their spears in front of my path, and I damn near end up kissing the steel before I manage to stop. *What the?*

The stern-looking guard on the left doesn't peer at me as he juts out his stubbled chin and speaks. "Apologies, highness, but the king wishes not to be disturbed."

I frown. Of course, there have been times when the king hasn't wanted to be disturbed in the past, but lately it's as if he's always busy. Not to mention that usually when the king wants to be left alone, he gives the guards an explanation to pass onto me. Going from the way these guards have their lips pressed tightly together, I'm guessing they've already given me the only explanation I'm going to get.

I think about returning later, but I can still picture Trey as he turned to ash, and the whole situation is making me uneasy.

"Did I say the word 'urgent'?" I say rhetorically, licking my lips. "Because I'm pretty sure if my father knew why I'm here, he'd want to see me right away."

Unsurprisingly, the guards still don't move and remain blocking my way like huge immovable statues. With the added height of their curved horns, they tower above me, but it's not like that makes a difference. Still, I wonder if it makes them feel foolish enough to think they can stop me. It always seems to be the largest demons who underestimate me the most.

"We have our orders, princess," the guard on the right replies this time. There's a scar that crosses over his lips, like someone once tried to cut down the center of his face, and my forehead creases more as I realize I've never seen him before. It's not like this is the first time the king has changed his guards. There are a few guards on rotation who I see the most regularly, but every now and then, I'll encounter someone new. Still, there's something about these two that has me on edge. I'm not sure if it's simply because I have the incident with Trey on my mind, or if my gut sense is trying to tell me something. Either way, a thread of panic winds through me. I know the feeling is irrational because King Dalton is the strongest demon to ever rule Seral and no one would be stupid enough to try and assassinate him, but...

Before the guards can react, I shoot my arms upward, flapping my wings to gain height as I knock their heads together with a satisfying thud. I'm careful not to use too much of my strength, just in case I've misread the situation, but they crumple to the floor unconscious, falling on top of one another in a tangled heap of limbs and armor.

"I did ask you to step aside," I mutter apologetically under my breath as I snatch up one of the guard's spears.

"Something tells me they're going to wake with bruised

egos more than anything else," Shade comments, peering down as I step over them.

"Unless I'm right about what's going on here," I reply. Because if I am, a damaged ego is going to be the least of their worries. *"Get ready,"* I send to Shade a split second before I open the double doors in front of me and burst into the room.

Time slows as I scan the space like a warrior scans a battlefield, ready to take down whatever threat has infiltrated the palace. I expect a witch assassin, or even one of the Drozac from the realm of the giants—trained killers who can harness their incredible strength while remaining in their smaller form—but instead of a warrior bent over my father's body it's...

"Ahhhh, I can't stop staring!" Shade shouts in my mind, flapping her wings and squawking in distress.

I cry out in surprise. I want to shield my eyes, but like Shade, my gaze remains glued to the figure who's bent over the bed with his naked body on display, his ass cheeks bare and his pants scrunched around his ankles.

"Why is it so red?!" Shade laments, her wailing commentary filling my head. *"Do you think he sat on poison ivy? Or is it some kind of allergic reaction?"*

My stomach roils as I notice the red welts climbing all the way up Dad's back. *"Stop!"* I plead to Shade. It's bad enough that I have my own thoughts to deal with.

"I'm just saying. If it is—"

I mentally block her from my mind to momentarily silence her, but it doesn't make the situation any better. As Dad sees me, he curses and scrambles to the side, almost tripping as he tries to yank up his pants. The physician standing behind him moves forward like he's going to help, but the king pushes him away, sending him flying across the room where he crashes into the wardrobe which splinters on impact.

My mouth opens and closes again as everything seems to happen at a comically slow speed. *Oops. So I did misread the situation.*

"Blake!" Dad shouts as he finally manages to do up his pants and rise to his full height. He's shoved his trousers on with such force that the fine material has torn at the seams along his legs, and I give him a sheepish smile as his face continues to redden.

His bare shoulders rise and fall rapidly as he peers at me, and then he turns his attention to the open doors. I'm guessing he doesn't notice the unconscious guards straight away, because he storms forward like he's intent on tearing their heads off for letting me enter.

Before he can pass me, I shoot my spear out, blocking his path with the blunt side of the weapon. "It wasn't their fault," I say quickly. I'm all for bloodshed when needed, but I'm not about to let the guards pay for my mistake. I mean, they *had* tried to do their jobs.

King Dalton blinks like he's only just seeing the guards on the ground, then his gaze lowers as he stares at the metal pressing lightly against his abdomen. There was a time when I wouldn't have dared to stop my father from doing anything. When just being in his presence would have made me tremble. At seven feet tall he's the largest demon in Seral and that's not even counting the thick black horns that curve over his head resembling a war helmet. He's the only ruler to finally lead the demons to victory against the witches. The only one who managed to unite the five realms against their common enemy, and the one who has fought for peace between the demon clans for more years than I've been alive. I can feel the physician watching us from across the room like an agitated bird wanting to fly away from here, but the doctor doesn't move.

"You had to know they wouldn't be able to keep me out," I say, shrugging apologetically when Dad still doesn't speak. Now that he realizes what's happened, I pull the spear away. "If you left a message with them, I would have come back later. But I thought you were being assassinated."

At that, Dad finally turns to peer at me, his black gaze finding my face. "Assassinated?" Seconds pass as he just stares at me, and then he jerks his head back and laughs. The abrasive sound rattles the walls like thunder, and slowly his anger fades, the tension leaving him like water disappearing down a crack in the pavement.

"She thought I was being assassinated!" King Dalton repeats, chuckling under his breath when his laughter dies down, and he shakes his head like the idea of him being attacked in his chambers is the most idiotic thing he's heard this century. Which, to be fair, it probably is.

His chuckle turns into a cough, and I narrow my eyes, watching him as he closes the doors. He's still coughing as he beckons me to follow him and leads the way to the black circular table in the middle of the room. A robe is draped over the back of a patterned armchair, and he pulls the material across his shoulders, wrapping it around himself, but not before I get another look at the massive red welts across his arms and back.

Letting down the mental barrier, I ask Shade, *"Have you seen anything like that?"* From her often surprisingly knowledgeable commentary, I sometimes get the feeling she's seen much more than she's told me about.

She sticks her beak out as she stares at the king with beady eyes. *"No. Is it possible he contracted a sickness from another realm?"*

A foreign allergen had been one of my first guesses, but as far as I'm aware, Dad hasn't left the castle in months. My gaze cuts to the physician as I follow my father to the table. As a general rule, demons don't get sick. With natural healing abilities, there aren't many things our bodies don't heal from. Because of this, there are few physicians in Seral, and most are usually called to help diagnose foreign illnesses and wounds that sometimes take longer to heal.

Before I can question the doctor, Dad waves his hand, dismissing the physician who scurries from the room like a startled mouse who's been freed from a trap. Reaching over, the king pours himself a glass of strong liquor from the bottle on the table and lowers himself onto one of the chairs.

I open my mouth, about to question him about the welts, but I snap my lips together when he commands, "Sit, daughter." From the tone in his voice, I know better than to argue.

Clenching my jaw, I drop onto the chair opposite him and cross one leg over the other. The back of the chair has been adjusted to accommodate my wings, and I stretch them out before folding them tightly again.

At first Dad doesn't speak as he watches me, but then he sighs, closing his eyes and rubbing the bridge of his nose like he's nursing a headache. "I'd planned to tell you at a more reasonable hour, but now that you're here, and given what you've...*seen,* I guess there's no point in waiting any longer."

I furrow my brow and lean slightly forward as I study his body language. I'm expecting him to deny anything is wrong, but from the way his usually proud shoulders are drooping down, I can tell he's already resigned himself to the idea that he's going to divulge the issue. I think he's going to tell me that there have been further setbacks with the negotiations between Seral and the royals of Rostof, realm of the giants. I expect him to explain that he caught a rash while visiting their realm in recent times, perhaps in secret, but he says, "Blake, I'm dying."

I don't hear him. Not really. I'm still busy thinking about the brutal Rostof royals, and his statement doesn't immediately sink in.

He continues to study me as he speaks. "When the rash started, I thought I'd caught an illness while I was away, but I've had multiple physicians visit me over the past months, and their diagnosis is always the same. The disease is mimicking the patterns of the sickness that took your grandmother centuries ago. I've always known that the battle with the witches would one day get the better of me, and it seems my time has come."

Seconds pass, and Shade speaks softly in my head. *"Uh Blake, did you hear what he said?"*

I swallow hard. "My grandmother?" It's the only thing I manage to say as questions fire through my mind. I think back to the history of my grandparents. My grandfather, King Xeron, was said to have died before the war against the witches, but my grandmother, Queen Ophelia, was documented to have died from a rare disease the physicians named, Witch's Burn.

During the war, the witches fought using all kinds of chemical weapons, and it's believed that these chemicals sometimes caused a sickness that inflicts irreparable damage to a demon's body. Once in a demon's system, the demon could live for years, centuries even, but eventually their body would succumb and lose the battle against the poison.

Emotion clogs my throat as I struggle to believe

what I'm hearing. "You're talking about Witch's Burn," I say, and when Dad nods, I protest.

"But that can't be right. You're over a thousand years old, and not everyone was exposed during the battle. If you had been, surely your body would have broken down by now." Research showed that once exposed to a particular cocktail of chemicals, most demons only lived another two centuries at most. I'd foolishly believed this meant the king was fine. "It has to be something else," I reason. I wish the physician was still with us so I could have studied his response to all of this.

King Dalton takes another drink before lowering his glass. I wait for him to crack a smile, but his brows are set into an unwavering hard line and, for once, I realize this isn't one of his games.

Shit.

"You're the rightful heir to the throne," Dad presses on as my mind begins to unravel, "but there are many who would try to usurp you. I've fought too hard for civility in Seral, and I refuse to die knowing it would crumble the moment Lady Fate takes me."

Lady Fate? From what Dad's saying, this doesn't sound like fate to me. This sounds like injustice. Anger rushes through me as his words sink in.

Dad's gaze softens as he stares at me. "And of course, like any dutiful father, I need to know you'll be taken care of when I'm not around."

His words cut through my anger, and my eyes begin to water, but I hold on to my emotions, keeping my expression unreadable. *Never show weakness.* It's the number one rule he's taught me since I was a child.

"You don't need to worry," I say, speaking past the hard lump in my throat.

He smiles, but his eyes shine with sympathy. It's a look I haven't seen on his face for years, not since I finally managed to get the demons to respect me, and I straighten my back.

"You've made a fine reputation for yourself as you've grown, daughter," he goes on, "but you're not..."

I wait for him to say any number of words that would fit at the end of his sentence. *I'm not what? A full-blooded demon? Cut out to be a demon royal?* These are all things demons have muttered behind my back since I was little. Well, they did until I showed them I was capable of making them scream and beg for mercy. Instead of uttering any of these things, he goes on to finish, "you're not powerful enough, yet."

I sit further back in my seat. *Yet?* "I'm stronger than any demon in Seral besides you." I retort. "If the clan leaders want to come for me and stop me from being queen, then let them." I've fought my whole life to prove I deserve the royal title that I was born with despite my angel blood, and to hear that I'm still not enough makes my heart harden that little bit more.

"I thought you don't want to be queen?" Shade asks, and I know she's trying to lighten my mood.

I don't answer her because she's right. I *don't* want

to be queen. But hearing that Dad still doesn't think I'm worthy to rule makes my jaw clench.

King Dalton raises a black brow. "While I am sure you would give them a fight, even you cannot expect to defeat all the clan leaders in your current state."

Wait. What? "And what current state would that be?"

He sighs wearily, and I wonder if he's tired because of the disease or because of me. "You're bondless, daughter," he clarifies.

"I'm..." When I realize what he's said, I laugh. "I can rule without being bonded. You're telling me that you're dying, and you want to discuss my love life?"

He rubs his thumb up and down the side of his glass. "While I'd like nothing more than to see you happy," he replies, "you know it's more than that. Without your bonds, you'll never achieve your full power."

"I'm already powerful," I say. "Just ask the demons I've trained with, or the ones who cower when they see me approaching."

"I'm not talking about being feared."

I don't hide my frustration. "Not all royals need to be bonded before their coronation. You weren't."

"I don't have half-angel blood," he counters, and though I try not to let it, the words still sting. I must fail at disguising my hurt because his expression softens again.

"I'm not trying to wound you, daughter. I love your mother more than life itself, and I remember what it was like before being bonded. How invincible I felt, but you will see. There is no greater strength than a demon with their bonded."

I know I shouldn't say it, but the words tumble out of my mouth anyway. "How can you say that after she left?"

I'm sure I've overstepped, but Dad's lips only twist into a smile. "I can say it, because when I bonded with your mother, I became the most powerful demon in Seral, and the time we spent together made the rest of my life seem dull in comparison. Most say that I'm the reason we won the war with the witches, but if I hadn't bonded with your mother, I'd be half the demon I am today." He pauses before he adds, "And I can say it, because she gave me you."

At his last comment, emotion threatens to overwhelm me again. *Dammit, Blake.* The king never says things like this. Sure, I've always known he cares in his own strange way, but he never outright *says* that he cares. The idea that he'll be gone soon presses down on me, making my chest ache.

I'm torn between arguing more about my bonds and saying something emotional when he rifles through the stack of papers sitting on one side of the table and pulls out a shiny red scroll.

His gaze locks onto me as he hands it over. "And it's because of you that I sent out these."

Confused, I take the parchment from him as a sickening feeling begins to stir in my gut. Usually when Dad says he's done something for me, I end up being put through some kind of test that he believes will build my strength or help shape my character. Like the fighting tournament where I'd had to compete against a few of the most skilled demons in Seral. I can still remember the look of pride on the king's face when I was the last one standing, bits of torn flesh hanging between my teeth and blood leaking from various wounds on my body. A chill slides down my spine at the thought. Mostly, because while the entire fight had been barbaric, I can't deny that I enjoyed making the competitors fall. In that moment I wasn't a half-angel freak. I was a demon, and I was to be feared.

But it doesn't mean I want to participate in another one any time soon. Carefully, I take the parchment and stretch it open. The red paper is trimmed with gold, and I recognize my father's cursive handwriting.

By invitation of King Dalton, ruler of Seral, victor against the witches, and protector of the demons, all unbonded alphas of the five allied realms are hereby requested to attend a royal ball. Whomever proves to be the fated mates of Princess Blake, heir to the Throne of the Kingdom of Seral, will rule by her side when the king retires after the twelfth full moon for this year.

Heat floods my cheeks as I go on to read that the ball will be held at the palace in a week's time.

"Please tell me this is a joke," I blurt, but seeing as

it's stamped with the official royal seal of King Dalton, I'm guessing it isn't.

"Invitations will be sent around Seral tomorrow, but scrolls have already been sent to Rostof, Kanzepes, Norso, and Toralyn," Dad replies mischievously, shattering any hope I have, and proving that he is as delusional as the invitation makes him out to be.

I think of Rostof the realm of the giants, Kanzepes the realm of the beast shifters, Norso the land of the water monsters, and Toralyn the realm of the angels, and I gape. "You're inviting everyone, including the giants? I'm pretty sure the alphas from that realm would rather see me dead than bond with me! Not to mention, the demons won't accept outsiders as their kings!"

"Show enough strength, and they'll come around. A union across realms might be just what we need."

"I always knew your father was sly, maybe this is a good thing?" Shade comments.

I shake my head, still in denial. "You can't think this is going to work?"

"Your mates are out there, daughter, and this might just be the way to find them. Considering your power now, once you've bonded you'll have the power to keep the throne of Seral, and I can die knowing I won't be leaving you alone."

There it is again. That aching pain in my chest. "And you're telling everyone that you're retiring?"

"I can't very well tell them the truth," he replies,

"but more may come now that they know you'll be taking the throne in a matter of months."

Ah, right. Because he figured they needed the extra incentive. After I'd won the last tournament, the demons in Seral respected me more, and in the weeks that followed a few would visit the palace, wanting to check whether they might be my fated. That is, until one of them ended up dead. He wasn't my bonded, but he was charismatic, and I was glad for the company. Well, I was until my vagina killed him. Or at least, I'm guessing it did. I'm not even sure what happened. One moment we were at it, and I was forgetting about life, and the next he looked like he was gasping for air until he died. Suitors stopped visiting the palace after that, and my reputation grew darker as rumor spread that I'd killed the demon for being terrible in bed. I'm pretty convinced that Lady Fate must hate me, and I'm destined to live alone.

"And your mates will need to be powerful to match you, so it's likely that they're alphas of their kind," Dad goes on.

I bite my lip. 'Alpha' is a word from the common tongue, used to describe the most powerful in each realm. For demons, this includes clan leaders, royalty, and any demons who have a strong gift. For some of the other realms, being an alpha is more biological. They're physically the strongest and largest.

"Not to mention three mates is the most common number of fated mates for a powerful female, so I imagine you'll have three or maybe even four," he continues to explain himself.

I think about my mother. She only had the one mate, *Dad*, because they both evenly matched each other. It's possible the same could happen to me, though occurrences like that are rare.

"I know you think you're doing what's best for me, but you need to call it off," I say, bringing my thoughts back to the events that happened earlier on in the day. "There's something going on in the city. The traitor I just interrogated was only a minor player in whatever is happening with the witches, and he had a weapon that turned his body to ash." My nostrils flare at the memory, like I can still smell the charcoal scent coming from Trey's horns. "We need to be focused on finding out what's going on, not organizing royal balls and inviting outsiders into our realm."

Dad doesn't look concerned. "It's one night, daughter, and finding your mates and unlocking your power will only help our situation. Until then, you have my blessing to do whatever you can to search out these traitors."

THREE

~ Princess Blake ~

The next week passes quickly, and I'm no closer to finding out about the witches' plans. When General Josek returned from the Fallon Blade clan house, he reported that it was empty, the rooms gutted and trashed, and even my crows can't find any sign of the clan members in the city. It's now the night before the ball, and the thought that I'll have to attend a lavish party to find my mates while we're still trying to figure this out has me feeling more irritable than usual.

I'm headed to the dining hall when an image pops into my head, a message from one of my crows spying in the city. While I can mentally speak to all of the crows in Seral, none of them are as conversational as

Shade, and most of them prefer sending me images when we communicate. I hope the crow has found one of the Fallon Blade clan members, but I'm surprised when I recognize the image of the front of the Coilan clan house with its massive palm trees and sprawling mansion that's built four stories high. The first picture is followed by another more graphic one, glimpsed through one of the mansion windows, and I mentally share the image with Shade who's perched on my shoulder.

"Great. That's just what we need," I grumble.

"Well, I have to give it to him. He does like to stay busy," she comments, her voice on the verge of laughter.

"It's only been three weeks since his last victim," I reply dryly.

"Maybe it's not what it looks like?"

Sighing, I turn around, heading away from the scent of roasted meat and caramelized vegetables. *"Something tells me it's exactly what it looks like."*

It's not long before I land inside the high brick walls of the Coilan clan estate, and I crack my neck as I fold my wings behind my back. Trees bursting with apricots line the stone path on either side of me, and the floral scent of jasmine mixes with the fruity scent. I breathe in the night air, my chest loosening. I've always loved apricots, often asking the palace chefs to include the stone fruit in their cooking. Stealing a handful from the trees when I leave is the only good part of visiting the Coilan clan house. *Later,* I mentally tell the apricots like I'm agreeing to a date.

Shade settles onto my shoulder, tucking her wings in tight. *"Do you think she's still here?"*

I cock my head, listening. *"Going by those faint moans, I'm going to say 'yes.'"*

My gaze sweeps over the grand mansion at the end of the path. Gray tiles cover the wide gable roof, and on the higher floors, balconies stretch across the building, vines clinging to the painted stone balustrades. This is the fourth time Shade and I have been here in the past six months, and at this point, the mansion is starting to seem way too familiar. I stride between the fruit trees and past a wide stretch of grass.

"You know, you could have let General Josek handle this," Shade jokes, and I'm surprised by how much the thought bothers me.

"We both know the general would have taken things too far. Especially after the other day." And by that, I mean General Josek would probably cut Dante's dick off to solve the issue here. As much as the Coilan clan leader is an ass with a knack for breaking the rules, he's a lover not a fighter. Taking the one thing he cherishes, possibly more than anything else, seems a little... harsh.

"Besides, I'm trying not to upset clan dynamics," I go on.

"Riiiight," Shade says, dragging out the word, though I'm not sure what she's implying. I ignore her, striding down the last section of the path and to the back door of the mansion. My stomach grumbles as I enter, the scent of apricots still strong, wafting through the open windows, and I chastise myself for not grabbing something from the palace kitchens to take with me. Ignoring the gnawing pain in my gut, I move along the carpeted hallway. We're passing eerily lifelike portrait statues when the moans and sounds of slapping flesh grow louder, reaching an almost fevered pitch.

I continue through a stone archway and move into the main hall of the mansion before I stop. In the middle of the room, on an excessively plush red velvet lounge, is a naked human on her hands and knees. Her face is scrunched with pleasure and her cheeks are as red as cherries as a male demon pounds into her mouth while another takes her from behind.

"You called it," Shade says with wry amusement.

The nearby armchair appears to be empty, but as I stare the clan alpha, Dante, materializes, his image solidifying until he's completely visible. He's dressed as he sits and watches the trio, but then his heated gaze slides my way. Warmth rushes over me at his stare, though I know the lust in his midnight blue eyes isn't because I'm here. The tournament from years ago pushes back to the forefront of my mind, and I remember seeing Dante's prone form, blood streaming from his ears. It had been a lucky hit, that one. When

I'd tossed another demon he'd crashed into Dante, smashing the clan alpha against the stone wall of the arena, and hitting him in just the right spot that Dante was instantly rendered unconscious. In the nights that followed, the clan alpha of the Coilan clan wasn't among the suitors who visited the palace. Not that I cared. He was an arrogant ass who bedded anything and anyone who showed him interest.

"Hmm well, she doesn't exactly look like she's in distress," Shade comments, still staring at the trio in the middle and bringing my thoughts back to the present.

"Rules are rules," I send back, though I have to agree. Honestly, none of the humans we've found here ever look like they're in pain. If anything, I always feel a little bad for breaking it up. But of all the civilizations, the human realm is the most fragile. The humans are also the most volatile and surprisingly dangerous despite their lack of magical abilities. Because of this, visiting the realm is forbidden unless absolutely necessary, like when I've had to hunt down errant demons. It's a rule that Dante has been ignoring of late.

"Our feared princess," the Coilan clan alpha says, his voice a seductive drawl as he lifts from his chair and strides toward me like I'm a party guest who's only just arrived. For a moment, I stare as I'm reminded of how beautiful he is. His midnight blue eyes and tall horns stand out against his jet-black hair, and the stubble on his face frames his chiseled jawline.

He's wearing black pants and a sleek black shirt that's rolled up to his elbows, showing off the intricate tattoos on his muscled forearms, and his tail flicks behind him as he walks. I stay where I am, watching him carefully as he gives me a devilish smile, because unlike the human in the room I know exactly what he is. Like him I'm a predator, not the prey.

"Dante, I wish I could say it's a pleasure to be back here again," I say with a humorless smile and plant a hand on my hip, though my pulse is beating harder than it should be.

He stops a respectful distance away, but his gaze travels downward as he appreciates every curve of my body just as brazenly as I admired him. At his back, the two males pull away from the human and quickly stand to the side of the lounge. "P-princess," one of them stutters as they bow their heads and cover themselves like they think I care if I see another naked demon. The female human lets out a noise of protest, but she quietens when she sees me, like she can sense something is wrong.

"Isn't it?" Dante asks with a mischievous grin. "I was sure you'd enjoy the view."

I narrow my eyes. "If you don't stop abducting humans I'm going to have to make an example of you. It's surprising word of your repeated transgressions with the humans hasn't already gotten out."

As always, he doesn't look the least bit remorseful. "Abducted? Camila summoned me," he defends.

"You know the humans aren't fully aware of

what they're doing when they summon us. They don't understand anything about our realm or our kind. You know better than to answer one of their calls."

He waves his hand dismissively. "Oh, some of them know enough. When I appeared in her room, she practically pulled me to her bed mumbling something about a smut lover's dream come true. I'm not entirely sure what that meant, but who am I to stop her from getting what she wants?"

I resist the urge to rub my temples.

"He's not wrong, you know," Shade chimes in. *"Not all humans think demons are terrible. There are romance books where the demons are—"*

"Not helping," I reply in a sing-song voice, cutting her off. It's only when Dante grins that I realize I've said it out loud.

I sigh, turning my attention to the human girl who's still staring at me from where she sits on the lounge. Her pupils are blown, and her cheeks are still flushed. Her gaze slides hungrily to the two naked males still standing to the side, one whom, I'm well aware is an incubus.

I tisk, clicking my tongue like I'm disappointed in him, though honestly, I'm not. It's hard to be disappointed in someone when they do the very thing you knew they would. I mean, the human summoned them and it's the equivalent of letting a fox into a henhouse and being angry at the fox for eating the hens. Occurrences like this happen more often than I like to think about, and as far as transgressions go, things could be worse.

The males flinch like they think I'm about to strike, and Dante steps to the side to block my view of them.

"Take her back, Dante, and make sure she remembers nothing of this," I say, pinning him with a stare. He looks like he wants to protest, but I continue. "And the next time this happens, I won't go easy on you. Honestly, I'm starting to wonder whether I should just kill you and get it over with."

His smirks like I've just whispered something dirty in his ear rather than threatened his life. *And this is what I have to deal with.*

My hands move like a blur, and Dante grunts as two of my blades sink into his chest. The human gasps, but Dante only keeps his midnight blue gaze on me as blood trails down his abdomen. I give him a withering stare until his smile finally falls. The wounds aren't fatal, and I know he'll heal as soon as he removes my blades, but I feel somewhat satisfied knowing they must hurt.

He clears his throat. "I'll return our guest," he agrees, and the human pouts behind him but doesn't speak.

"I mean it," I tell him. "If I have to return, next time I won't show mercy."

His eyes darken, and I hope it means I've gotten through to him. I glance at the human girl and the other males one more time before I turn to leave. I'm at the doorway when he calls out, his voice like a seductive caress that reaches across the room. "I'll see you at the ball, princess."

I pause only for a heartbeat, and then another blade is in my hand. I twist, letting it fly toward Dante where it pierces into his chest, just beneath his heart. He grunts, but the playful smile gracing his lips doesn't shift.

"I'll be the only female there," I remind him, not sure why he'd bother attending when it's clear we'd be terrible for one another, and Lady Fate wouldn't possibly match us.

He only continues to stare at me, those dark eyes fixed on my face. "I'm counting on it."

I scowl and don't say another word as I leave the room.

CHAPTER

FOUR

~ Princess Blake ~

The next night, I sit straighter on my throne ignoring the bite of the cool black marble beneath me as the string quartet to my right plays a haunting melody. I've opted to wear a black corset dress paired with skintight black pants, and a curved dagger is strapped to my thigh, mostly because I felt too naked without my weapons. I tap my blood red nails against my wine glass as the guards follow the king's command and open the doors of the grand ballroom. There's some kind of commotion that I can't see, but then a horde of demons, shifters, archangels, and other monsters stream in, all dressed in finely tailored suits and embroidered tunics depending on what realm they're from. Hundreds have turned up, and my chest tightens as the cavernous room fills quickly.

"Is the king expecting you to dance with all of them?" Shade asks, sounding more excited than horrified. She's perched on my shoulder, and she swaps legs tucking the other one into her feathers to keep warm against the chill in the room. *"You know, I'm not bonded either, and I'll happily volunteer as tribute if you need a hand. If they turn out to be my mates, then you'll know they can't be yours."*

I force myself not to grin. *"I'd swap with you if I could. Though..."* I pause thoughtfully, *"do crows even have mates?"*

"Sure we do," she chirrups. *"But it's usually only one mate, and we don't actually bond or do anything fancy like that."*

"And I'm guessing your mates also aren't usually a demon or some other monster?" I add.

"That, too, but hey, I'm willing to give anything a shot. I'm here with you, aren't I?"

This time I can't hold in my smile. *"And thank Lady Fate for that. I can't imagine having to go through this alone."*

She ruffles her feathers and swaps legs again. *"Anytime, girl."*

A resounding thud echoes as the guards close the massive ballroom doors, and I pay attention to the alphas. The majority of them remain in segregated groups, sticking to those of their own kind. Palace servants weave between the guests, offering drinks from their silver trays laden with glasses.

The alphas from Rostof, realm of the giants, are the easiest to identify. The largest in the room, the giants all reach at least seven and a half feet high. Black tribal tattoos cover their thick muscled bodies, and many of them have braided beards decorated with beads. Their long hair is kept neatly away from their rugged faces, and most of them are wearing some combination of leather clothing. It's been a long time since I've seen a giant in the flesh. Like the beast shifters, they're able to change their forms at will, except instead of changing into massive animals and other creatures, giants can increase their size three-fold. If one of them were to take on their giant form in here, it wouldn't end well, but the king would take care of them before that happened. And so would I, for that matter.

More than one of the giants is glaring at me, and I hope Dad knows what he's doing by bringing them here. The last thing we need is an incident with the giants when our relationship with the royals of Rostof is already fragile.

"Well, they look like a friendly bunch," Shade comments, clearly noticing them as well. *"You still think the king's hoping you'll bond to one of them?"*

"All of the Rostof princes are already bonded, but if I'm mated to a giant who's a well-respected member of the royal court, it would be an easy way to build trust between our realms," I reply. *"I don't mind who my mates turn out to be,*

as long as I can unlock my power and stop the demons in Seral from destroying themselves." At that, I tilt my head, staring at one of the giants who is talking animatedly to a male beside him. I can't help but wonder what the sex would be like with such a large male. I mean, would it...fit? An image of the demon I bedded, the one who ended up dying pops into my head, but I try to push it away. That wouldn't happen to my mates...would it? It was a problem I'd have to figure out another night.

"Whoa, maybe stay away from that one," Shade says, distracting me. *"That guy with the cloak looks like bad news."*

I swing my gaze to where a cloaked male is standing among the giants. I can only make out his vivid gray eyes, straight nose, and square jawline that's covered with stubble. His hate-filled glare makes my skin prickle with awareness, and I resist the urge to reach for my dagger. The giants move around as they chat to one another, and the alpha disappears into the crowd. *"Great. I knew Dad made a mistake by inviting the giants."*

Keeping my chin high, I try to forget about my new hate club, and turn my attention to the group from Norso. Their realm is made of ninety-percent water with huge sea creatures that roam the seas, moving in territorial pods. The alphas from Norso are distinct with thick strands of green and blue hair that reminds me of seaweed, and angular features that are accentuated by the shadows in the ballroom. I've heard their kind also has webbed toes, which helps them glide through the water when they're swimming with the sea creatures, and it makes me wonder how different the rest of their bodies are.

Truthfully, it's not something I ever thought I'd have to contemplate. I always assumed my mates would be demons, or that I wouldn't have any at all. Suddenly it all seems so...complicated.

I turn my gaze to the shifters from the beast realm, Kanzepes, next. They appear to be just as hostile toward me as the giants. I wonder if it's because their ruler, Queen Nareen, had once propositioned King Dalton. From what I've heard, she didn't take it well when she found out they weren't fated mates as she'd believed. The relationship between our kingdoms has been tense ever since.

All of the beast alphas are in their non-shifted forms, dressed in earthy-colored tunics, but half of them are looking at me like I'm their dinner, while the other half are staring at me like I'm some kind of prize. *Well, this is going to be fun.*

Between the different groups, demons strut across the ballroom floor, their pristine suits gleaming in the dim light. The demon alphas act like they own the space, and from their arrogant expressions it's obvious that more than one of them thinks they're going to be my fated. *I guess mentioning that the king will be retiring soon really did work wonders on their attitudes.* Dante is among them, his hair sleeked back, and a pristine black suit fitted to his athletic body. Undoubtedly, if this were a different party, she-demons would be falling all over him. He grins and winks at me, and I avert my gaze, not wanting to encourage him. The last thing I need is him making a spectacle in here. It's incredible the mischief a demon can get into when they have the power of invisibility.

"Who is that?" Shade practically squawks in my mind, distracting me, and I turn my attention to where she's staring.

Standing in the middle of a group of archangels, is a devastatingly handsome male with thick golden locks, a sculpted symmetrical face, and a heart-stopping smile that has my breath catching in my throat. Even his lips appear to be brushed with gold. His golden armor shines under the lights coming from the great chandelier suspended high above him, intricate swirls and whirls cut into the metal covering his chest and shoulders, and large feathered golden wings are folded behind him. *Merciful Lady Fate.*

"That would be archangel Prince Callan from Toralyn," I answer, still staring at the male who has a golden crown nestled in his hair. Most of the princes from the other realms are already bonded, and truthfully, I'm surprised the prince attended.

Shade sticks her beak our further as if she's trying to get a better look at him. *"Well, can I just say that he already has my vote."*

"Of course, you'd pick the male with wings," I tease.

"Yeah, and the body of a god," she sends back.

I roll my eyes.

She hops onto her other leg. *"So, what's the plan?*

The king thinks when you dance with them, you'll just know if they're your fated mate?"

I ponder her question as I recall everything I've been told about fated mates over the years. What is the first sign again? *"Well, if they're your fated mate they're supposed to smell irresistible,"* I answer.

"So, you're dancing with them to see if they stink?"

"What, no. I mean, they're supposed to smell so good your mouth waters, and you know they're yours." Okay, so I'm doing a crappy job at explaining, but that's probably because I can't actually imagine any kind of scent that would have that effect on me. Well, maybe if they smelled like chocolate? My lips twist into a slow smile as I think of one of my mates always smelling like sugar and cocoa. *Yes, please.*

Shade paces on my shoulder. *"Wait, so you're going to have to smell all these guys?"* She sounds horrified, and honestly, when she puts it like that I kind of am too. *"I take it back. I'm no longer volunteering as tribute."*

I grin. *"It's not just that,"* I go on, trying not to think about whether some of the males will smell like body odor, or worse. *"They're supposed to taste good, too."*

"Taste good?" Shade questions, and had she been a demon, I would have imagined her raising a curved eyebrow.

"I don't know," I admit. *"I'm just reciting what I've learned. Also, when you're close to your mates, Lady Fate's magic is supposed to pull you together. Like you want nothing more than to be close to them."* My lips quirk up

at the sides. *"Oh, and I think you're also supposed to have some sort of an emotional connection."*

There's a moment of silence before she recites, *"So you need to smell them, taste them, and then..."*

"Bone them," I finish unashamedly. From everything I've read, most know that they're fated before it comes to this, but having sex is a foolproof way to check if you're mates.

Shade grows silent again for a while, and I know she's staring out at the sea of alphas who are laughing, drinking, and gawking at me. No one has approached me yet, and I wonder if it's simply that no one wants to be the first to ask me to dance. Likely, they don't want to be the first to be rejected.

"Out of my way you feathered freak!" a gruff voice draws my attention, and I watch as a giant smashes his shoulder into one of the archangels as he passes. The blow sends the archangel with bronze wings staggering to the floor. Before the male can get up, the giant sneers and spits a wad of yellow phlegm onto the archangel. It hits the male between the eyes and slides down to the tip of his nose and hangs there. "You look better already," the giant laughs. "But I still think the only good angel is a dead one." He turns away but his smile falls and he shouts a curse when a burst of wind lifts him high into the air. Prince Callan strolls casually forward, and the fallen archangel lifts to his feet as the giant shouts a stream of slurs. His face grows redder as he moves his arms and legs like he's still trying to walk in mid-air, and I have to suppress my smile. The music in the ballroom stops.

"Put me the fuck down!" The massive male flails, bellowing and raging. None of the other giants go to help their comrade. Though, that could possibly be because the demon guards along the walls now have their spears pointed forward like they're readying themselves for a bloodbath.

I copy King Dalton's position, leaning back and relaxing on my throne though the rock-hard marble is anything but comfortable.

"Wow, I had no idea this night would be so entertaining," Shade chirps like she's eager to see the show. *"What an asshole."*

"I said let me down!" The giant screams.

Prince Callan's lips twist into a dark smile. "As you wish." With the flick of his wrist, the wind stops swirling around the giant. There's a second where the male remains suspended in the air, but then he crashes to the stone floor. A distinct crack echoes through the room as one of the giant's legs breaks, the shattered bone puncturing through his skin.

The giant grunts in pain as he cradles his injured leg. "You fucking psycho," he spits.

"Aren't we all," Prince Callan drawls with a bored expression. "Now, apologize to Theon, and then beg the princess for forgiveness before I get any other ideas."

My mouth pops open in surprise, but I press my lips together quickly. I figure he must be joking, but he's staring at the giant with such sincerity that I soon realize he's serious.

"Mmm, sexy and commanding," Shade muses. *"Did I mention that he has my vote?"*

I have to admit I'm impressed, but the thought of bonding with an archangel makes my stomach tie in knots. I've made it a point never to go to Toralyn, realm of the angels. That way, it's easier to pretend that side of me doesn't exist.

The giant gapes at Prince Callan like he's sure the archangel has lost his mind, then he turns his attention to the giants watching from across the ballroom. Despite their grim expressions, no one goes to his aid. *Guess he's an asshole to his own kind, too.*

Realizing that none of them are going to help, his jaw ticks and he jerks his head toward the archangel, Theon, who's standing there with an amused expression. "I apologize," the giant snarls through gritted teeth, but there's hatred in his eyes like he's imagining creative ways to kill the archangel.

Prince Callan flicks his wrist again, and the air moves around the giant making his body twist and putting pressure on his broken leg. The giant cries out, pain contorting his features. "I fucking apologized already!" he yells.

Prince Callan stares at him with a blank expression. "Like you mean it," he says calmly.

The giant's cheeks puff, his right eye twitching, but he turns to Theon again. "I *sincerely* apologize," he says this time.

Prince Callan nods and smiles with approval. "And now the princess. You insulted our future queen, and you'd better hope she's merciful."

The giant's eyes flare wide. "B-but, no I didn't mean—"

"She's half angel, is she not? Do you wish her harm?"

The giant stutters, realizing his mistake. "N-no, of course not."

My own cheeks burn. I've never associated with the angels, and I just assumed they would detest my mixed blood just like the demons. *Was I wrong?*

"Whoa. In the human realm angels are always portrayed as being placid and kind," Shade comments. *"But this guy is giving off some serious badass vibes."*

I don't know much about the human realm beyond my most basic studies, but 'kind' isn't the word I'd use to describe angels. From what I've heard, they're just as brutal as the rest of us, though they do tend to frown on injustice.

The giant cries out again, and I'm guessing the archangel prince must be inflicting more pain because the giant's expression quickly changes. "Stop," he begs, his rough voice cracking. Turning his gaze to me, he blurts, "I deeply apologize your highness." He slides his gaze to King Dalton, then back to me again. "I misspoke. I swear, I meant no disrespect."

For a moment, I think I glimpse the hooded male with the gray eyes watching from somewhere among the group of giants, but he's out of sight again a second later.

My heart pounds as I feel the weight of the golden crown on my head, and all gazes turn to me. *Well, that's just great. I guess it's back to rule number one of being a demon royal: Never show weakness.*

"*Go put pressure on his broken leg and do that staring thing you love,*" I tell Shade. "*I'll send some friends to join you.*" I don't want her in harm's way, but at this point I'm sure the giant wouldn't dare hurt her.

"*Aye aye, captain,*" she chirrups back and launches from my shoulder. She flaps her wings, rising high into the air as I tap into my power and send out the mental call. Energy rushes through me making my body tingle, and I look up, waiting until dozens of crows fly through the high up window that I always leave open. They fly around Shade, matching her movements, the birds curving around the ballroom and swooping down until they reach the giant. One of them perches on his head, while the others stand on his limbs and on the floor around him. Shade lands directly on his broken leg and hops around. She's not heavy, but even that pressure makes him grunt. To his credit, the giant doesn't move to shake them off.

Shade stops to stare the giant in the eye, and the other crows do the same. His face pales.

"*Want me to caw?*" she asks, "*or do we need to peck him bloody?*"

I scan the ballroom, taking note of the tense

expressions around the room. *"I think cawing will be enough."*

She opens her beak to caw, but that's all it takes. The giant flinches and blubbers another apology. Satisfaction goes through me. I discovered early on that crows make monsters superstitious. They say when a crow caws it means something ominous, like an impending death. Now all I have to do is ask Shade to caw in the right situation, and monsters start falling over themselves in fear. I'd think it was pathetic if it wasn't so damn handy. *"Perfect. That will do."*

When the giant continues letting out a stream of apologies, I make it a point to sigh exaggeratedly. "Enough. I accept your apology." I could take the giant's life for his disrespect, but then we'd have a mess to deal with. "Let's get on with the party!" I say, making a show of flicking my hand as if it's a commanding gesture to my crows even though I don't need to, and on cue, Shade flies to my shoulder while the other crows fly back out through the high window.

"Great work," Shade says, peering out at the alphas. *"That was all you."*

The band starts playing again, and the alphas resume chatting and mingling with one another. Happy that the situation is resolved, Prince Callan gestures to an archangel with electric blue hair and tan skin. The archangel moves toward the giant, and when he reaches out his hand, the giant's leg heals, the bone moving to its rightful place and the skin smoothing over. It's well-known that giants don't heal like demons, and I watch in fascination as the giant is made whole again. *Huh. So angels can be kind.*

The giant is quick to jump to his feet, and he doesn't so much as look at the archangels as he returns to his group, careful not to brush past anyone else.

With the drama over, King Dalton gestures with his hand, and the guards along the walls move back into their usual standby positions. I can't stop staring at the archangel prince. Prince Callan is nothing like I expected, and honestly, I'm a little impressed. I knew the prince was powerful, but I didn't know he was honorable. As though he can feel my stare, he turns my way, his golden hair flicking over his eyes. As our gazes lock, his entire face transforms, his captivating smile entirely at odds with the violence swirling in his penetrating eyes, and I find I can't look away. *Oh, boy.*

"Dance with him first," Shade urges. *"Something tells me he's going to smell real good."*

Fuck, I hope she's right.

~ Nate ~

I maneuver through the crowd, moving past the other alphas as they jostle one another in the ballroom. An archangel stretches his wings in front of me, unknowingly blocking my path, and a brown feather floats to the ground as I step around him. The urge to take a bite out of one of the archangel's pretty wings has my teeth turning into fangs, but I force myself to behave. I'm not here to cause trouble. Besides, from the sounds of things, someone else already has that covered.

Up ahead, I soon see who's causing the commotion. A giant shouts a string of curses from where he remains on the floor, nursing his badly broken leg. The sickeningly handsome Prince Callan stands over him, watching the giant with a calm expression as he orders him to apologize for whatever he must have done. *Glad I'm not that fucker.*

King Dalton had to know that bringing so many alphas together was going to cause chaos, and I'm sure this is only the beginning of what will be an immensely entertaining night. Which is great news for me, because I'm relying on the fact that there will be more distractions in the hours to come.

Hidden amongst a group of archangels who are watching the scene unfold with the giant, I scan the room, taking note of the closed exits, the thin balcony that curves around the ballroom, and the floor-length windows that run along the left side. There are fewer demon guards on the balcony, and I quickly map out any number of routes I could use to make my way up there.

When I heard of King Dalton's invitation, I'd been one of the first in Kanzepes, the beast realm, to register my attendance. It didn't matter that I'd already been planning a heist for months, with the intention of relieving one of the wealthier families of their most prized artwork. Years ago, I'd heard a rumor in Kanzepes that the king holds a treasure which he took from the witches during the war. A power so great, the demon king himself is afraid to use it. I figure something like that must be worth an unimaginable sum, and it's hidden somewhere within these walls.

There weren't many in the beast realm who could tell me much about the demon palace aside from the fact that it's known to be built like a fortress, but the royal ball is the perfect distraction allowing me to get in and out. Unfortunately, I hadn't expected the sealed steel doors down each of the corridors, and the sheer number of demon guards who are lingering in every shadow, but it's not going to stop me.

It's only then that I realize the room has grown silent, and the giant is no longer on the floor. I look around, following the gazes of the archangels around me.

Well call me a kitten and take my treasure. I blow out a breath, all coherent thought stolen from me as I finally let myself look at her. I'd been avoiding staring at the princess, not willing to let myself be tempted, but now I can't help but admire her.

Hello gorgeous. The demon princess sits with her head held high, her golden gaze vibrant against the thick kohl that lines her eyes, and her porcelain skin contrasting against her plump red lips. Thick raven-colored hair cascades in waves over one shoulder, and a dress made of leather and lace hugs tight to her body, showing every curve. She's smaller than I thought she would be given her reputation, but her black-feathered wings drape behind her throne, making her seem imposing, and there's something wild in her golden eyes that makes my entire body respond.

The rumours about her being attractive do not do her justice, because the female is beyond beautiful. She's downright breathtaking. A purr starts in my chest, low and possessive as my creature decides to stake a claim, but the rumbling ceases when I realize who she's looking at.

Of course, it's him. I glare at the asshole with the golden wings and winning smile. If she's interested in Prince Callan, then this female isn't my mate. She can't be. Besides, Lady Fate would never match us. I'm a low born from a part of Bazlen City that the Kanzepes royals like to pretend doesn't exist. King Dalton may have invited low and high born alike to this ball, provided they were able to prove their strength and power, but someone like me isn't meant to be a royal.

Nonetheless, I'm tempted to step from behind the cover of the archangel in front of me. To expose myself and see if the princess swings her golden gaze my way, but I don't. Instead, I allow myself a moment to fantasize about what I could do with those perfect pouty lips of hers, and my body tightens at the thought of this female on her knees before me. I've heard rumors that Princess Blake slaughtered her last lover for being incompetent in the bedroom, but that doesn't worry me. I've never heard a complaint yet. I think about returning to Seral in the future and stealing into the princess's bed. About how I would make her scream and claw at the sheets with those deliciously long nails as I fucked her, my hands tangled in her silky hair.

Fuck. I curse myself for getting swept up in the fantasy. *How long has it been since I've had good company? Months?* I was going to have to fix that when I made it back to Kanzepes.

Princess Blake is still staring at the archangel prince, and I can't help but wonder if Lady Fate has a sense of humor. What would it mean if I turned out to be one of the princess's mates? If I were, I'd get to rule in Seral by her side. But while the idea of sharing the delectable princess makes my mouth water, I know I'm not cut out for life in a castle. *No, I'm only here for the treasure, and I'm not leaving without it.*

With my mind refocused, I turn my attention to the long balcony that overlooks the party. This is likely the trickiest location I've worked with, and even after I make my way from the ballroom, navigating around the palace itself is going to prove to be difficult. *Not to worry, if I run into trouble, well, it's a good thing I still have my nine lives.*

~ Princess Blake ~

"Welcome to all of you who have come here today," King Dalton's booming voice fills the ballroom, and I snap my gaze away from Prince Callan. I hadn't even noticed the king stand, but now he addresses the crowd with his glass raised.

"I want to start by thanking you for attending and

showing your interest in my beautiful daughter." Dad turns to stare at me, and my cheeks warm under his scrutiny. It always unsettles me when he's being unusually polite.

"I fear, I have kept her busy these past years," he continues. "Too busy for her to entertain any thought of finding her own mates, but I'm hoping this will soon change. As I detailed in my invitation, those who turn out to be her fated will rule over Seral when I retire after the last full moon for this year."

Dad pauses, staring down the males around the room. "If you're here it's because you are an unbonded alpha who has yet to find your mate, but if you wish to rule Seral, you must prove you are worthy of my daughter. Showcase your skills, demonstrate your strength, and above all else, survive. Then we shall see whether Lady Fate has determined that you are to be bonded."

"Wait, what? I thought I just had to dance with them all and see what happened?" I send to Shade. I start to wonder whether the alphas already know of this new development, but they all look as confused as I am.

"Maybe he's expecting them to engage in hand-to-hand combat?" Shade suggests.

"Find the provisions left at the major landmarks around the city if you hope to keep your wits about you," Dad continues, proving Shade's suggestion wrong. "But tread lightly or you may never return."

What does that mean? Dad smiles when he turns to me. With his crisp black suit and the golden crown circling his head encrusted with jewels, it's easy for me to forget about the disease that's slowly taking him. "Remember, daughter, Lady Fate doesn't make mistakes. Not when it comes to your fated. Find your mates and survive." He's barely finished speaking when he slides a black mask over his face and gray smoke begins puffing from seemingly nowhere.

The music continues, the haunting tune reaching a crescendo like the notes are taunting me, and I cough as I inhale the smoke. *Ah, crap. I really should have seen this coming.* The alphas let out startled curses, and I hear glass shatter right before the world turns dark.

CHAPTER
SIX

~ Princess Blake ~

My eyes feel like they're full of sand the next time I crack them open. Blinking slowly, I try to get rid of the gritty feeling and groan at the stiffness in my limbs. My head throbs, and I massage my temples as I stare blearily into the sunlight around me. *Find your mates and survive.* Dad's last words are like a warning as they repeat in my mind. I think about killing him the next time I see him, then feel guilty because the male is already dying. *What the fuck is he thinking?* Now more than ever, he needs me, but of course, Dad wants to use this as an opportunity to put me through one last ordeal to see whether I'm worthy of the throne. Except this time, I'm not the only one being tested.

At that thought, my heart skips a beat, and my eyes snap wider as I search around me. My fingers run over the flat stones of the courtyard, but my feathered friend isn't here. *"Shade?"*

Panic squeezes my chest, but then a black blur swoops from above. *"I'm here,"* Shade replies, landing on the stones before me.

Relief makes my shoulders sag. *"Are you all right?"*

She tilts her head to the side, observing me. *"Are you?"*

I stretch out my arms and peer down at my body. I'm still wearing the black dress I had on at the ball, but I appear to be unharmed, and thankfully, my dagger is still strapped to my thigh. My crown isn't on my head, but I'm guessing Dad was smart enough to keep that at the palace. *"I think so."*

"I'm fine, too," she replies. *"I woke an hour ago and took some time to scout over the city. The alphas have been transported in groups, but many of them are awake now, and some of them are trying to make their way to you. I guess they think you're the only one who can get them out of here, and their best chance of surviving is if you're mates."*

Lifting to my feet, I wobble as I take in the thick gray clouds now above me instead of the vaulted ceiling of the ballroom. *"And where exactly are we?"* I stumble back a step as I take in the crumbling buildings surrounding us. The ancient structures reach high, many without a roof, and their uneven walls are like broken fingers trying to reach for the sky.

"Perstalia," I whisper, answering my own question. "The ninth realm." I tick off the realms in my head. There are the five allied realms, Seral, Rostof, Toralyn, Kanzepes, and Norso. Then there's the realm of the witches, Larazeen, which we'd thought was uninhabited until recently, the human realm, Earth, and the shadow realm, Kiru, where our souls reside after death. Perstalia is the ninth realm, otherwise known as the lost realm. There are tomes in the palace library that speak of the winged creatures who used to live here and a civilization that rivalled even that of the angels.

The courtyard is empty except for Shade and me, and I turn to the stone wall on my right which is decorated with a long mural. Roughly cut pieces of colored tiles have been artfully arranged, and I walk beside the picture running my fingers lightly over the dusty depiction of a beautiful landscape with a great river and trees dotting the sides of a riverbank. White crystals are embedded between the tiles, and they sparkle in the watery sunlight as I brush away the layer of dirt. *Whoa.*

"What is this place?" Shade asks, perching on my shoulder.

"The beings of Perstalia were said to be made of magic," I reply. *"But while they were powerful, they were defenceless when the witches invaded. They hadn't encountered beings from other realms, and the witches fed off the magic of the land and the creatures for decades, depleting every resource until there was nothing left. Not*

even plants will grow here now. It was after Perstalia was left in ruin that the witches turned their sights on Seral. Our land isn't as magical as Perstalia, but we're similar because the magic of our horns was fed back into the land when we died." I wonder then, if Perstalia would still be a thriving civilization if we'd known about their realm sooner. My heart squeezes as I reach the end of the mural, and I pause to study the ancient stone buildings around us.

"That's so sad," Shade comments, tucking her wings in tighter even though the air is warm.

"For the last two centuries, these ruins have become neutral ground for the allied realms," I explain. *"Any major council or negotiations that involves all of the leaders of the five realms are held here in the ancient castle. But that still doesn't explain why Dad sent us here. There's nothing here besides the destroyed buildings, and remnants of their lost civilization. Not to mention it's well known that the witches poisoned this land. If we're here for too long, we'll lose our minds."*

"I'm sorry, but lose our minds? You didn't want to lead with that last part," Shade complains.

I shrug a shoulder. *"I've never been here long enough that I've had to worry about it. The last time I was here was for negotiations years ago, before we met, and we only stayed for a couple of hours. We'd have to be here for quite a while to be affected."*

"Well, considering all the king said was "find your mates and survive", I think it's safe to say that we could be here for some time."

I frown, knowing she's right. "*Which is why he instructed us to find the provisions left at the major landmarks around the city if we hope to keep our wits about us. He planned for it. There's a drug you can consume that staves off the illness. He must have left some of it with the provisions. It's all part of the challenge. We just have to make our way to the closest landmark.*"

"Hold on, even if we do find this drug, there are hundreds of alphas in the city. What if there's not enough to go around?"

I grimace. "*I guess that's where the 'survive' part comes in.*"

She swallows. "*Okay, easy peasy. So, we survive until you find your mates, and wait until dear old daddy comes to get us. Then what? Bam! Back in Seral?*"

I sigh. "*Knowing the king, we're completely on our own until he comes to check in. So your guess is as good as mine.*"

Taking a moment, I try to mentally visualize a map of the ancient city in my head. I can count on one hand the number of times I've visited Perstalia. Usually, I never leave the royal castle, but the last time I was here, I was able to take to the sky and fly high enough to glimpse a main square with a huge fountain that no longer flows, and a series of bathhouses that are clumped together in the south. I think of the other alphas then. My mates might be in the city, but there's also a whole bunch of alphas who *aren't* my mates, and I'm willing to bet there are a few who will happily keep any provisions for themselves.

"You said you saw some of the alphas?" I ask Shade. I'm aware that the sooner I find my mates, the easier this will be, especially when I unlock my power. It's said that fated mates have a deep connection, and that if they're close, Lady Fate will draw them together. I'm not sure how close they need to be, but Dad obviously thinks that if we're all together in this city they'll be able to find me. But getting our hands on provisions is a priority.

Shade preens her feathers. *"Yes, some of them are closer than the others. In fact, one of them should be almost here."*

Wait, what? I'm about to question her more when a flash of green catches my eye, and an alpha from Norso comes into view, striding between two stone buildings on my left.

"Thanks for the heads up," I grumble to Shade in disbelief.

"You're welcome!" she chirps, not caring that I'm entirely unprepared for this encounter. *"He's handsome, isn't he?"*

I stand taller and observe the male walking toward me. Like the other alphas from Norso he has sleek features, a lean muscular body, and a green vest made of tiny seashells. His thick green hair reaches his shoulders, the strands swaying as he walks, and the moment he sees me, his lips curve into a smile.

"Ah, demon princess. I'm glad to have found you." He speaks in the common tongue as he approaches, walking with a confident gait.

I peer around, half expecting more alphas to be behind him, but he shakes his head. "Just us," he says with a thick accent. "All the better for me." His cheeky smile widens, and he stares at me like he thinks we're already mated.

"Attractive and confident," Shade observes. *"I like him."*

"You like everyone," I counter, then quickly block her from my mind because I'm not going to be able to have a conversation with this guy while she's in my head.

"You look happy for someone who was just gassed and left in Perstalia," I comment, honestly amazed that this guy looks so calm. With Dad, nothing surprises me anymore, but this has to be a shock for the alphas.

He shrugs. "It does not matter to me as long as I still get you."

My brows lift. It's obvious this guy has forgotten that we don't get to choose our mates, but I'm happy to indulge him for now. Who knows, maybe he *is* my mate.

As he reaches where I stand, he stops and dips his head. "Because you, my dear, are as beautiful as the brightest pearl in the ocean."

I smile politely. I'm not sure if 'bright' is a word I'd use to describe myself, but I have to say, I'm feeling pretty good about him right now. *And Dad thought this was going to be hard.*

"Thanks," I reply. "So how should we—"

The air squeezes from me as he grabs my hand unexpectedly and spins me until I hit his hard chest. *Oof!* Shade flaps into the air, dislodged from her perch, and the male's strong arms slide across my body. Maybe it's because of his pearl metaphor, but I have the distinct thought that his arms are like the sides of a clam shell closing me in. Instinctively, I want to elbow him in the ribs, but I restrain myself. He's obviously convinced we're mates, and they do say fated mates can have odd responses to one another when they first meet. Still, I'm about to tell him to take a step back when I smell him, and I freeze. *Merciful. Lady. Fate.*

He smells *terrible*, and not just in a musty kind of way. As I inhale, I choke on the scent of sweaty socks, sea salt, and rotting fish. It's like I'm smelling something that's been left at the bottom of a sea barrel for months, and it takes all my effort not to gag.

Wincing, I push lightly against his hold, but instead of taking the hint, he only grips me tighter and drops his nose to my hair as he sniffs *me*. I scrunch my face and wait for him to realize we're not fated, because surely, I must smell bad to him too if we're not mates, but he only murmurs something appreciative under his breath. *What the fuck?*

Shade paces at the top of the mural wall, watching me intently, but I shake my head at her, not wanting her to get involved.

"Look, I get that you wanted this, but it's not

meant to be," I say quickly, still trying not to breathe in.

The alpha stills, and I think he's going to let me go, but then he says, "No, we are fated. You will see. I have waited for this." His head lowers like he's going to kiss the side of my face, and...that's the extent of my patience. *Fucker.*

My elbow slams into his ribs with enough force that I hear a satisfying crack, and he stumbles backward. Spinning, I turn as he curses and his expression changes, fury reddening his pale-green features. "We are fated. I will make you seeeee—"

His last word rings in the air as Prince Callan steps up behind him and tosses him into the air, using wind power to send him sailing above the tops of the nearby buildings and out of sight.

I'm so bewildered, that for a moment I simply continue to stare at the empty sky, but then I snap my gaze to the archangel prince who's now standing in the alpha's place. Anger flashes on Prince Callan's face but it's gone quickly, and his expression smooths.

Shade lands on my shoulder, and I'm sure she must be internally ranting about the fact I didn't let her help, but I can't worry about that now.

"I was about to handle that," I point out matter-of-factly as I watch the prince.

He dusts off his hands, and his lips curve into a devastating smile. "Yes, but why should you have to?"

I blink, stunned. In Seral, I often have guards close by, but they never act unless I ask them to. As a demon royal, punishing the demons who disrespect me is a show of strength and is expected.

"Because it was my fight," I say when I manage to get my mouth to work.

He only shrugs like he did the obvious thing, but then his brows lower, his forehead wrinkling as confusion floods his features. "Oh, you're serious. Would you like me to retrieve him so you can punish him yourself?" He spreads his wings as if to launch after the alpha who's probably splattered on a sidewalk on the other side of the ancient city.

"What? No," I splutter, but I don't think he's heard me. "Stop," I say, shooting forward and resting my hand on his broad shoulder to prevent him from flying away. Before I can think about what I'm doing, his scent envelops me, and my heart begins to race. He smells like sunshine after it has rained. Like warmth, and the cool crisp sky as I soar through the clouds. He smells like the sweet tangy scent of green apples with hints of bergamot. "Oh, shit," I whisper. It's so at odds with the dark, musky smell I'm accustomed to back in the palace, but my body responds, need rushing through me as suddenly all I can think about is this male spreading my thighs. His muscular body moving... *Whoa, hold on. What the fuck?*

I go to step back, but his head jerks my way, and I stand frozen as his throat bobs, his body stiffening under my hand. "My *Ahalian Touizda*," he whispers low with a thick angelic accent that makes my knees weak. Tingles rush over me, and it's not because of what he's said, because I have no idea what that means, but it's the *way* he's said it. Like I'm his... everything.

His hooded eyes drop to my lips, and my breath hitches, but just as I expect his lips to slam against mine, he takes a large step away from me. My hand falls from his shoulder, and a coldness that I've never felt before spreads through me.

His expression changes, his arrogant but charming demeanor replaced with something much harder. "This wasn't supposed to happen," he mutters, and I reel back. They say when you find your fated mates the bond is irresistible. I guess not.

"I'm sorry, but isn't this the whole reason you're here?" I say, the coldness inside me turning into anger. "To find out if you're my mate?"

His jaw tightens. "You're a princess, you know what it's like. We all have our obligations."

Obligations? I scowl. "So what, you thought you just had to attend the ball, prove that we're not bonded, and go on your merry way?"

He runs a hand through his golden locks. "Something like that. And King Dalton better have my crown tucked up somewhere safe in Seral palace, or there's going to be a world of trouble if I return to Toralyn without it."

I force myself to let out a long breath.

Shade ruffles her feathers and squawks, and I activate the magic that allows me to speak with her, pulling down the mental barrier.

"Finally!" she says in my mind. *"Do you want me to peck his eyes out or go for his balls?"*

Her voice is exactly what I need to hear, and it takes the edge off my anger, if only a little bit.

"I've got this," I reply, though for once I'm not sure if that's true. Traitorous demons I can handle, but a mate who doesn't want me... I struggle to keep it together and try not to think about his scent of green apples and bergamot that's still lingering in the air even though he's moved away.

"Look, whatever is going on here, I need all my mates to seal the fated mates bond so I can unlock my power," I say, trying to remind myself that in the end, that's all that matters. "After we're bonded, you can go back to Toralyn and forget I even exist." My stomach twists at the thought, but he's right about one thing. We all have our obligations, and making sure Seral doesn't fall is mine.

He glares at me like I've just insulted his existence. "No."

My mouth pops open. "What? But we're *mates.* If we don't bond, it's not only me who won't be able to unlock the rest of my power. You won't be able to, either, and if I have other mates out there, neither will they."

"Like I said, girl, eyes or balls?" Shade comments, and I'm half tempted to take her up on her offer.

"I'll stay with you until this ordeal is over, but then I'll be on my way," he says.

"But—"

"You're not mine!" he snaps harshly, his words burying as deep as any blade could.

For a moment, I can't breathe. Pain lances my chest, and it's so unusual, so unexpected, that it takes all my effort not to double over. *Not mine.* The words ring in my head, cutting deep, even though I hardly know the prince. I know it's because he's my mate, but that knowledge doesn't make it hurt any less. Grinding my teeth, I fight against the urge to sink my dagger into one of his perfect eyes. Because this isn't just about me...

Never show weakness. Seems the rule also applies to fated mates. "Fine," I say, feigning indifference.

"Blake?" Shade questions. *"But if he doesn't bond with you, you won't get your power, and neither will your other mates."*

"I figure at least if the prince is with me, I can make sure he doesn't die," I explain.

"Oh, good point. Plus, he'll change his mind when he realizes how awesome you are."

I'm not sure about him changing his mind because of me, but I'm hopeful I'll be able to convince him to bond eventually. I have to. I pin Prince Callan with a stare. "Tag along, but don't expect me to come crawling when you realize you fucked up."

The corners of his lips twitch up ever so slightly, and he rasps, "I'd never expect you to crawl." The words are quiet, and there's something sensual about them that makes my heart pound faster, but then as if he realizes what he's said, his lips flatten.

Desire rushes through me, but I push it back down. I've lived my life having to deal with the king's games. I'm not about to let Prince Callan toy with me.

Giving the archangel my back, I speak to Shade. *"We should find some provisions."*

"You mean, you need a distraction so you can stop thinking about this ass?"

I blow out a breath. *"Something like that."*

She twists her head to the right. *"There's a theater a few streets to the south. Do you think the king has planted something there?"*

My feet are moving before I answer. *"Let's find out."*

~ Princess Blake ~

"I still think you should have let me give him a piece of my mind," Shade grumbles as we make our way through the ruins with Prince Callan following behind. The housing is denser here, the homes right up against one another, and there's something about this place that makes me feel like I'm being watched. The back of my neck prickles and I'd rather fly, but until we get provisions, I decide it's better if we don't draw attention to ourselves.

"I'm angrier at Lady Fate for picking wrong," I reason, bringing my thoughts back to the prince. I wonder then whether he already has a lover back in Toralyn. I've never heard of any relationship getting in the way of a fated mate bond, but then again, I'm new to all this. The thought of Prince Callan with someone else makes my stomach churn, but I try not to think about it.

"Maybe Lady Fate doesn't know he's such a huge asshole," Shade suggests. *"Because you're amazing! He should be worshipping the ground you walk on."*

I grin at that, and the delicious image of Prince Callan kneeling before me with his wrists cuffed enters my mind. I'm practically drooling when I shake my head, trying to dispel the image. *Dammit. Stupid fated mate bond. Keep it together, Blake,* I chastise myself. *The prince has flat out rejected you, and you still can't help but fantasize about him.*

"He's lucky he helped you out with that guy from Norso," Shade prattles on, *"or he'd be returning to Toralyn with only one eye."*

I stop walking, my boots stalling on the flat stones as I remember how he'd helped me recently, *and* how he'd dealt with the giant in the ballroom. Despite what the prince just said to me, my anger cools a little at the thought.

Prince Callan must be as distracted as I am, because he almost walks into my back. He steps to the side in time and stops beside me. Clearing his throat, he peers at the crumbling stone buildings lining the street. "Where are we headed?" It's the first he's spoken during the time we've been walking.

"There's a theater not far from here," I explain, though I don't point out that I only know this because of Shade's scouting session earlier. "If I'm right, the king has left provisions there. I figure it's a good idea to get our hands on at least one of the packs before the alphas find them."

I start walking again, and another few minutes passes before Prince Callan asks, his casual demeanor back in place, "Is this normal for you? Being gassed by your father and left in less-than-ideal circumstances?"

I think about snapping at him, but what would be the point. "We have a complicated relationship," is all I say in response, and thankfully, he doesn't ask more.

We walk the rest of the way in silence, not encountering any other alphas until we reach a large circular building made of stone and decayed wood. It's two stories high, with a balcony along the top floor, and little square windows that look to the outside. When we fly above the building, I notice the middle of the structure is open, and I'm able to glimpse an expanse of bare sand that surrounds a stage in the center of the space. As I'd hoped, a black box trimmed with red sits on the platform.

"There it is," I mutter under my breath.

Prince Callan hovers in the air beside me, staring down at the theater. "You do realize that's a trap, don't you?"

I keep my eyes fixed downward. "If I'm right, that box contains the medicine we need, and I'm not leaving here without it."

"I figured as much," he replies. Reaching down, he unsheathes a broad sword with an intricate golden hilt that perfectly matches his gleaming armor.

"What are you doing?"

"Collecting the box. Didn't you say we need it?"

I narrow my eyes. "Yes, but—" Before I can finish, he drops into a dive, swooping low so fast he's down near the stage in a matter of heartbeats.

"Callan!" I hiss after him, trying not to raise my voice. *Great. First my mate doesn't want me, and now he's about to die.*

"Uh, what does he think he's doing?" Shade asks, flapping her wings beside me as I fly after him.

"I wish I knew."

It's too late for me to stop what's happening, so I only watch as Prince Callan nears the box. His large wings flap steadily as he hovers before the box, not touching it straight away as he scans the theater. I look around us as well, noting the shadows clinging to the wooden beams.

I have no idea what kind of surprise the king has left here for us. In the past, I mostly endured physical challenges, but something about this place has me on edge. I try not to think about what will happen if Prince Callan really doesn't survive this. Before I can call out a warning, the archangel leans down, scooping up the box with his free hand. I brace, ready to swoop down and fight, but the theater remains silent.

Prince Callan beats his powerful wings harder, rising again with the box pressed against his chest, and for a moment, I think I must have misjudged the situation. It wouldn't be the first time. Years of unexpected trials and challenges have clearly made me paranoid.

I grin, relief coursing through me...and then the sand erupts.

~ Nate ~

I drop my nose to the street and a low rumble starts in my chest as her delicious scent fills my senses again. Like a beacon, it draws me toward an abandoned circular building that reminds me of a smaller version of the stadiums we have in the beast realm. I stare up at the dilapidated building. *Hmm, why here, princess?*

I'd woken in the city some time ago, and after getting over my initially wounded pride at having been blindsided by the king, it wasn't hard to guess King Dalton's intentions. The demon king is known for his games, and this city is like a giant maze with his daughter as the end point. I'd opted to explore the city in my beast form, and it hadn't taken me long before I'd scented her, the mouthwatering smell of honey and cinnamon making my beast purr and leading me here. A flash of black wings draws my attention to the top of the building, but they're out of sight soon after, and a thunderous hissing and clicking sound makes my ears twitch as the ground shakes.

"Callan!" a panicked feminine voice calls out, her husky voice making my body coil, and I bare my teeth as a primal urge to protect thrums through me. It took some time for me to admit it to myself, but after following her scent for a good while in the city, I slowly had to acknowledge that my compelling desire to find the princess wasn't just because I knew she was my ticket out of here. The female is my *mate.* Bonding to the demon royal doesn't exactly line up with my life plans, but for now I figure it could prove to be advantageous. If she stays alive, that is.

Leaning back on my haunches, I leap halfway up the side of the building, my claws digging in as bits of wood and stone fall to the ground. The clicking and hissing from inside the structure grows louder, and I move quickly, scaling the wall until I reach the roof. There, I crouch on the tiles, peering over the edge as my tail flicks with agitation.

In the middle of the space, giant insects slither from a wide expanse of sand. There are at least half a dozen of them, their long-segmented bodies and countless legs allowing them to move with frightening speed as they swarm the area and attack Prince Callan and Princess Blake.

Demon bugs. I recognize the ugly fuckers from a job I once pulled off along the border of Seral. They usually reside in the wild and only attack if you harm their offspring. *And here I was hopin' I'd never have to see them again. How King Dalton managed to transport them here is beyond me.* My slitted eyes watch the sand, and I know all too well how bad things will go for me if I leap down there.

Hovering a few feet from the ground, Prince Callan blows back a bug before swiveling to pierce his sword vertically through the head of another. Not far from him, Princess Blake moves fluidly through the air, spinning as she drives her fist through a bug's head, then uses her dagger to slice at another one's belly. Yellow ichor sprays over her, but she doesn't flinch as she takes down the insects one after the other, moving with lethal grace like she's danced this dance a thousand times.

Together, the royals take down the last bugs around them, and like it has been timed, the creatures fall to the ground, unmoving on the surface and not sinking into the sand.

Prince Callan smirks and holds up the strange black and red box he's been cradling this whole time. "Now that's over, shall we get out of here?"

Princess Blake grins, but her smile falls as the ground begins to tremble again, the sand bubbling up as creatures move beneath the surface. The crow flying around them squawks in panic, and Princess Blake's gaze narrows on the box in Prince Callan's arms.

"They must be in there!" she shouts, realization taking over her features as multiple massive bugs burst from the sand, the creatures even larger than the last ones. Their clicking and screeching grows louder as they rise higher toward the hovering figures.

Before Prince Callan can react, one of the bugs

swings its head into him, sending him flying into a wooden beam. The wood splinters on impact, and he rolls, narrowly avoiding the insect as it strikes again, its head smashing into the destroyed beam.

"Callan, let it go!" Princess Blake yells as she holds back another bug. Her dagger is no longer in her hand, and she braces against the beast, stopping the creature from puncturing her with its venomous fangs.

My muscles tense as the primal need to protect is like fire in my veins. I drop down onto the next floor, my paws light on the wooden slats of the balcony, but the structure groans from the weight of my massive body.

Princess Blake curses as one of the bug's legs slashes across her cheek, drawing blood, and the scent of honey and cinnamon grows stronger in the air, all but sending my creature into a frenzy. She lets out a cry as she tears the insect apart, and it takes all my willpower to turn my attention back to the archangel.

Prince Callan dodges to the side, narrowly missing another strike, and as the insect draws its head back, preparing to attack again, I leap for him. My teeth scratches against the archangel's armor as I take the box in my mouth, wrenching it from his muscled arm and falling to the sand below.

My paws sink on impact, the ground rippling beneath me, and I vaguely hear someone's sharp cry as I'm pulled beneath the sand.

CHAPTER
EIGHT

~ Princess Blake ~

The acrid smell of the demon bugs is all over my body, but it doesn't stop his scent from reaching me. As the giant jaguar leaps from the balcony, his long paws outstretched toward Prince Callan, his musky, earthy smell reaches my nose, making my head spin. I'm in a daze as he snatches the box away from the archangel prince, and then he's landing on the sand.

"No!" I shout, diving for the male who could be my mate, but it's too late. One of the bugs pulls him down, the clicking in my ears growing louder as he disappears below the sand. *Crap!* It's the first damn trial I've encountered since arriving in Perstalia, and I'm already failing. The remaining insects disappear after him, and the theater becomes eerily quiet again.

I plant my feet on the wooden slats to the side of the sand, on the ground floor below the main roof, and Prince Callan settles beside me. "He snatched it out of my arm," he says like he thinks I'm upset that he lost the box.

When I don't respond, he follows my gaze to the sand right where the beast shifter disappeared. "I always knew Nine Lives would die while stealing something, but I never imagined it would be like this."

I jerk toward him. "Nine Lives?"

Prince Callan nods. "That's what the angels call him. He's a well-known thief in our realm, and he's escaped death more times than I can count."

A thief? Is that why he stole the box? I mean, I'm not judging, I just hadn't expected it. From what I've heard of the beast shifters, they're heavily driven by pack loyalty and honor. I stare back at the sand like I think he'll emerge any second, even though I know it's impossible.

Shade perches on my shoulder.

"I think he's my mate," I tell her and let out a dry humorless chuckle because this is beyond believable. My first mate doesn't want me, and my second mate is about to die stealing from me. I always guessed Lady Fate must have a sense of humor, but this is ridiculous. I brace, waiting for the pain. It's said when you lose one of your fated mates, bonded or not, you feel their loss as unimaginable pain, and even when the feeling

subsides there's still an emptiness inside you reminding you of their death for the rest of your life. And if he's my mate and he dies before we've bonded, there goes my chance to unlock my power.

"Are you sure?" she asks.

I keep my gaze fixed on the sand. *"I guess I'll know soon."* I'm actually surprised it's taking this long for the shifter to die now that the bugs have him. There's no way he could fight that many. There's no way—

The sand shifts not far from where we stand, and my heart stutters.

"We should go," Shade says quietly as I prepare myself to fight, but I can't leave until I'm sure. Not until—

A massive paw breaks through the sand and my heart almost stops. One paw becomes two, and soon the entire furry beast is in sight. The giant cat shakes its muscular body, sand clouding the air, and his earthy scent of the forest makes my pulse race. Slitted reddish-gold eyes lock onto me, and I stand captivated as I take in the pattern of rosette spots covering his body.

"Like I said, Nine Lives," Prince Callan mutters with a smirk. "I shouldn't be surprised."

The jaguar tosses an extra-large leather-wrapped bundle to my feet, and gestures with his head for me to open it.

I bend down, feeling the creature's gaze on me as I untie the leather straps and unfold the material. *What?* My gaze snaps back to the shifter. "It...It's the supplies," I say in disbelief. In hindsight, I should have known the red and black box was only a decoy because it was nowhere near big enough to fit the weaponry, provisions, and other items now in front of me. "How did you—"

I swear I see the cat smile, and then his body shifts, the fur disappearing and his limbs reshaping until it's not a beast but a man standing in front of me. He's as tall as Prince Callan, but with tan skin and lean muscle that makes my heart pound. With a defined jaw, those distinct reddish-gold eyes, and shaggy reddish-brown hair accompanied by dark brows, he is...delicious.

My body reacts to the sight and scent of him, and he gives me a playful smile that makes my insides melt. "The bugs usually only attack if they're defendin' their young," he says, and I blink, reminding myself that he was answering my previous question.

"The chest was filled with eggs, wasn't it?" I ask, knowing full well that I must be right.

The male nods. "Once they were returned, the bugs were happy to go back to guardin' their unhatched rather than attackin'. They shouldn't bother us now." He gestures to the weaponry and other supplies at my feet. "That was in their nest. I figured you must have been after something considering the way the, uh, prince here was determined to hold on to those eggs."

"In my defense, I didn't know there were eggs inside," Prince Callan points out.

"Gosh, Blake, I hope he's a shower and not a grower,

because if he's your mate I'm scared for your vagina," Shade's voice breaks into my thoughts, and I cough as I struggle to keep myself composed. Unable to help myself, my gaze lowers.

"Holy Lady Fate, what is that?" I hiss back at her. My question is actually serious, because the anaconda I'm looking at can't possibly be his penis. It's huge, and I've seen a few hung demons in my time. *"I mean, is that a shifter thing?"*

Prince Callan clears his throat beside me, and I'm pretty sure the anaconda is starting to get hard while I stare, so I lift my gaze only to see the shifter's shit-eating grin.

"I blame you for that," I send, and Shade's crowing laughter sounds in my head.

"Oh phew, he is a shower," she comments with amusement, clearly still staring. *"I really was worried for a minute there."*

I would strangle her if it wouldn't look so damn odd. *"Stop staring,"* I hiss, and she only laughs again.

Great. "Anyway, thanks for that," I say to the stranger. "Uh—"

"Nate," he replies, that arrogant smile still on his sexy-as-fuck face. "My name's Nate. And if I'm not wrong, I think we might be fated."

The breath rushes out of me at his blunt statement.

"May I?" he asks, holding out his hand. He brings my fingers to his lips, his whiskers scratching my skin as he presses a kiss to my hand, sending a chill down my spine. "It's my honor, my queen."

"*Your Queen?*" Shade swoons. "*I hope Prince Callan is taking notes, because Nate is so much better at this.*"

"Honor?" Prince Callan scoffs, oblivious to Shade's commentary.

Nate lowers my hand and slides his slitted gaze to the archangel. The hatred between them is palpable, and I narrow my eyes at them.

"Okay, clearly you two have some kind of history, so will someone tell me what's going on here?" I ask.

Prince Callan glares at Nate. "The last time I saw Nine Lives was when he was in a cell for trying to steal the prize jewel of Toralyn from the palace. He'd been scheduled for execution the next morning but mysteriously disappeared from the dungeons."

"And the last time I saw you, you were spurtin' some bullshit about redemption," Nate retorts.

"Right," I say, eyeing them both. I've never been a fan of drama, and whatever is going on between them is already giving me a headache. "So, you really are a thief?" I ask Nate.

"I was," he admits, and then his eyes light up, his gaze heating as he stares at me. "But it seems destiny now has other plans."

Suddenly my clothes are making me feel much too hot, and my body tingles at the attention.

Prince Callan laughs darkly. "You couldn't handle ruling a kingdom."

"Well, I guess I'm goin' to have to prove you wrong. *Again*," Nate retorts. "I'm willin' to bet I'm goin' to enjoy being a king *very* much." His heated eyes are still fixed on me, and my pulse races at the way he's staring. Like he's imagining taking me in every position. Or maybe that's just what I'm thinking. I become keenly aware of how naked he is, all rippling muscles and tan skin.

I bite my lip, and he tracks the movement, his alert gaze watching me like a predator watches prey. Only... I'm anything but prey, and he's...

I drop to my knees abruptly and begin bundling up the supplies and tying the leather straps.

Neither of the guys say anything, but I can feel their eyes on me, and the smell of them has my inner muscles clenching.

"*Blake, what are you doing?*" Shade asks in a sing-song voice. "*It was just about to get interesting. At first, I thought you were getting on your knees to give Nate some lovin', which was unexpected and might have made you look a little desperate, but you're packing up? C'mon girl.*"

"*Prince Callan has already made it clear he doesn't want me, and Nate is a famous thief. Who knows what he wants.*"

"*Your v-a-g-i-n-a,*" Shade says, dragging out the word 'vagina' like I'm an idiot. "*It's pretty obvious what that pack of muscles and fur wants. Just look at his—*"

I heft the bundle of leather onto my shoulder. "*I killed my last lover, remember?*" I say cutting her off.

"*Yes, but he wasn't your mate.*"

I ignore her. I know she has a point, but I just can't deal right now.

Nate is watching me curiously, a playful grin back on his face, and Prince Callan is staring at me with casual indifference.

"The demon bugs might be appeased for now, but I think we should get out of here," I say, then not waiting for either of them to reply, I spin on my heels and lead the way out of the theater. I hear the males following behind me, and when we're on the street I keep walking.

"You know, you're going to have to sleep with them to seal the mate bond," Shade points out. *"If they truly are your fated mates, nothing bad is going to happen when you're with them."*

"That's just it, isn't it?" I reply. *"I don't know for sure."*

She twists her head to peer back at the guys. *"I saw the way Nate looked at you. You could have fun with him first to loosen up. Going by the way he's staring at your ass right now, I'm pretty sure he's down."*

Heat flushes my cheeks as I imagine myself climbing onto Nate's face, but I banish the thought and let out a long breath. *"Not yet. Let's just get some medicine into our veins and find my other mates first."* I'm not sure how I know I have more mates out there, but I have this feeling, this emptiness, like I haven't found them all yet.

We walk in silence for a while until tingles spread along the back of my neck. I peer at the surrounding buildings, half expecting to find someone watching me.

"*What is it?*" Shade asks, staring at the buildings as well.

I focus for a moment longer on a structure with two floors and gaping holes where the windows used to be, then I turn my attention back to the street. "*Nothing. It's probably just the ghosts of the past haunting us.*"

"*Ghosts?*" she snaps back, a tremor in her voice.

I grin. "*You know I'm only teasing. This isn't the shadow realm.*"

"*You sure?*" she says, flicking her head fearfully from side to side. "*Because you could have fooled me.*"

I shake my head. "*How did you ever survive without me?*"

"*Uh, worms and seeds. Small talk with other birds who flew by the windows. Bad TV and listening to smutty audiobooks that my humans used to play?*"

"*Exactly,*" I chuckle, then blink as my vision becomes unfocused for a moment. "*Crap, I'm guessing this place is starting to get to me. We need to get that medicine into us.*"

CHAPTER

NINE

~ Princess Blake ~

Far from the theater, we find an abandoned building to set up camp for a few hours. I'm guessing it was once someone's house, but there's no roof, only four stony walls and two massive holes where doors used to be.

Dropping the leather bundle onto the ground, I unfasten the ties and sift through the contents. There's a single weapons belt that I strap around my hips, then I slide a sword and two daggers into the sheaths already feeling more like myself. Sitting amidst the waterskins and multiple parcels of food, is a small black-leather pouch, and I open it to find four bright orange pills.

"What are the chances they're actually poison?" Shade asks from my shoulder.

Her comment makes me think of the traitorous demon, Trey, but these pills are distinctly different, the color matching the pills I've taken when I have visited Perstalia in the past.

"Let's find out," I reply and pop one into my mouth, chasing it down with water from one of the waterskins. She stares at me like she's waiting for me to explode, but seconds pass, and I grin at her. Breaking one of the pills into quarters, I hold out a piece on the flat palm of my hand. She pecks at the pill, her throat bobbing as she swallows it.

Turning, I hold the pouch out to Nate and Prince Callan. "Unless you want to start hallucinating, take one of these each." Prince Callan grabs the pouch first and eyes the pills dubiously before tossing one into his mouth. Nate takes the other one, and I grab a set of clothing that was included with the provisions and throw it his way. He plucks it out of the air and pulls on the t-shirt that's sizes too small, and pants that only just fit over his insanely sculpted ass. I'm not sure if Dad put them in there intended for me, but Nate grins, posing in the clothing that shows the bottom of his defined abs.

"What do you think?" he asks me, mischief sparking in his eyes.

Prince Callan looks at Nate like he thinks the shifter is an embarrassment, but he doesn't comment.

I smother a smile. "It's an...improvement."

Abruptly, Nate moves beside me, crouching to pluck a bottle of wine from the provisions and popping the cork as he stands again. "Oh, yes!" His throat bobs as he takes a swig, then he pulls the bottle away from his mouth and lets out a satisfied sigh. "Now I understand why you were so determined to get this."

"And the medicine had nothing to do with it?" Shade says sarcastically as she watches him.

He smacks his lips together, his eyes fluttering closed. "Mmm, I can even detect notes of wood smoke. I'll have to tell Dad he has good taste when we're back in Seral."

I almost choke on my own spit. *Dad?* Standing, I face Nate who opens his eyes and gives me a playful smile. "We can't even be sure we're mates yet," I say as the thought of him calling King Dalton *Dad* makes me queasy.

Still grinning, he takes a large step forward until he's only inches from me. *Crap, he smells good.* His scent is addictive, the hints of the forest making my chest loosen and my body warm at his close proximity. The urge to unashamedly breathe him in makes me swallow, but I don't move as he lowers his lips close to mine. "Then, my queen, let's find out, shall we?" he purrs, and a low rumble sounds in his chest, the possessive noise making my breath hitch. He waits there like he's expecting me to move the rest of the way and claim the kiss, and my body responds like he's everything I've ever needed. His lips are a hairsbreadth away, and my mouth waters at the idea of tasting him. At the need to claim him and confirm that he's mine.

But my muscles lock up as I refuse to let myself move toward him. They say when you find your fated mate you know instantly. That Lady Fate will be there, pulling you together, and winding the threads tighter between you, but...my fear of hurting my mate is still there cutting through my impulse to claim him, and there's more to this shifter than meets the eye. This male has secrets, and I need to find out what they are.

My tongue feels like lead as I say, "The bond won't seal into place unless we're all present. We should find my other mates first."

"*Girl, I'm not even his mate, and even I want him,*" Shade's voice sounds breathy in my mind. I'd actually forgotten she was still on my shoulder.

Nate frowns. "How can you be sure the prince and I aren't it? I won't speak for Callan, but I'm not exactly...weak, so you might only have two mates. We should test the theory."

"*He has a point,*" Shade chirps, sounding way too eager.

"*Pervert,*" I mumble at her.

She only laughs in my mind.

I think about telling Nate that I can somehow tell that I have more mates, but instead, I turn my head to where Prince Callan is leaning against the wall with his arms folded across his chest. The archangel will shut this down. "And what do you think?" I ask, sounding bored. "Should we find out?"

Prince Callan's lips start to curve as his eyes heat, but then he stops himself, his brows forming a hard line. "No."

Hearing that one word stings just as badly as the first time he'd rejected me. I force a smile to my face and turn my attention to Nate. "There you go."

Nate's mouth opens and closes. "So we can agree that he sucks, but that doesn't mean we're not your only mates." He fixes a glare on Prince Callan. "If we bond, it might get us out of Perstalia faster."

There's something in the look they share that makes me feel like I'm missing something, but Prince Callan flicks his hard gaze to me. "Is that true?"

I shrug. "Probably not. My guess is that the king is planning to check in on us in a few days or a week. Who knows with him."

Prince Callan nods once and pushes off from the wall. "I'm going to keep a perimeter watch. We don't want any unmedicated alphas sneaking up on us... unexpectedly." He stares at Nate as he says it and disappears through one of the doorways.

I clench my jaw, cold rushing through me as he leaves. *Thank you, Lady Fate,* I think sarcastically. *Why did I have to get a dud mate?*

Determined to distract myself, I snatch up one of the parcels of dried bread and move to a wall, sliding down until my ass hits the stone floor. Shade flies to the ground and hops over to the provisions in the leather satchel. Amongst the parcels of food are scattered seeds, and she pecks at them hungrily.

"Your Dad is going soft in his old age if he's also leaving food for me," she says happily.

"He only put them in there, because he knows I would make his life miserable when I return to Seral if he didn't," I point out.

"Then you've trained him well," she chuckles.

Nate stands there for a moment, and then he moves to the opposite wall, sitting down to face me. The bread is tasteless in my mouth, even though I know Dad packed the good stuff. I know it's not going to quell the hunger that swirls in my stomach.

"And I always thought the archangel prince was just a prick to me," Nate mutters, staring at the doorway where Prince Callan disappeared and taking another drink of wine.

"So what's his deal?" he asks.

At first, I think he's still referring to Prince Callan, but then I notice his predatory gaze is fixed on Shade. She ruffles her feathers, and his slitted eyes remain locked on her.

"Uh, Blake. Can you please tell your new kitty that I'm not on the menu," Shade says, a wobble in her voice.

With my free hand, I have one of my daggers out in an instant. Flicking my wrist, I send it flying across the room. As expected, Nate grabs the dagger out of the air, just as the second dagger I throw lodges between the stones near his head.

The red in Nate's eyes deepens, and he gives me a feral grin.

I smile sweetly back at him. "Shade is a *she* and if you so much as touch a feather on her back, I'll let her peck your eyes out." I stare at him for a moment longer, then go back to eating my bread, because I need something in my mouth to distract me from the delicious-smelling shifter sitting across from me.

There's movement through the doorway on my right, and I glimpse Prince Callan's dark smirk before he disappears again. I'm glad he was eavesdropping, because that's a warning I needed the prince to hear as well.

Nate puts down his bottle and smiles. "Don't worry, gorgeous. I wouldn't dream of eatin' your friend," he says, and this time his predatory gaze isn't on Shade, but on *me*.

"Fuck it, tell him I am on the menu. He can have me," Shade comments.

I squirm in my leathers, feeling the heat from his gaze. I'm tempted to just give in, but the moment I think about climbing onto Nate's lap, I picture the demon I'd killed. I remember the way his face became pale, his eyes bulging as he gasped for air. I've killed my fair share of demons, but they always deserved it. But that night was different. *It can't happen to my mates...can it?* I'm still lost in thought when Prince Callan calls out, "We've got company."

Nate and I are both up in a heartbeat. Nate pulls over the leather flap, covering the provisions as I stalk outside to find Prince Callan standing with his sword out, watching four alphas who are striding down the narrow street toward us. From their stature and their leather clothing, I'm guessing they're shifters, and they're all swaying a little on their feet. One of them has blood on his brow, and another is limping, his ankle twisted at an odd angle.

At the sight of me, they grin broadly.

Nate steps up on my other side. "Well, they look…"

"Like shit," Prince Callan finishes.

"Do you know them?" I ask Nate.

He shakes his head. "Can't say I do. But I'm guessin' by their sluggish movements they're starting to feel the effects of this place." He sniffs the air. "Looks like we have a couple wolf shifters, some kind of reptilian shifter, and…" he sniffs again, "a bear shifter."

"Okay, well some can be affected by this place faster than others," I say. "Though, no one knows why."

As the alphas get closer, I assess each of them. Despite looking a little rough, they're all reasonably attractive, but it's hard to tell whether I have a connection with any of them.

"Demon princess," the male on the far right says when they all stop a couple paces away from us. "We've finally found you."

Unlike the other three shifters beside him, this guy is unusually hairy with thick bulging muscles, and I assume he's the bear shifter. His brown gaze roves over me appreciatively, and both Prince Callan and Nate tense at my sides.

"I'm glad to see you're faring well so far," I say, though it's clear they didn't find any of the king's provisions.

"As well as can be expected in this place," the shifter replies gruffly, a hint of irritation in his voice.

I don't blame him for being annoyed. I'd be salty, too, if I were them.

"Cut the niceties," Prince Callan drawls like the shifters are wasting our time. "You're here because you want to know if you're her mate. Let's get this over with so you can be on your way."

The shifters all glare at Prince Callan, and I do the same. He doesn't even blink when I look his way.

The bear shifter clears his throat, and I pivot back in his direction.

"Princess, let us be your kings and we will treasure you forever," the shifter says.

"*Well, that's romantic,*" Shade comments, and I have to agree.

I circle around the alphas, then step close to the bear shifter who grins as I move toward him. He lifts his hand as if he intends to slide it behind my back, but I shake my head, a sympathetic smile on my face.

His jaw ticks, his grin falling, and a frown takes over his face. "What? You can't know already; we haven't even touched."

But unfortunately for him, I do know. I'm still standing a foot away from him, and he doesn't smell right. The scent of bleach and soap wafts from him, and it's taking all my effort to stop from wrinkling my nose. The long-haired alphas beside him don't smell any better, and instinctually, I just want to move away from all of them.

"We don't need to touch," I reply. "You're not my kings."

One of the other alphas protests, and he reaches out, grabbing my hand as I pass. Nothing sparks through me at the physical contact. No desire, only annoyance that the alpha has grabbed me when it's obvious I don't want him to.

I feel Prince Callan and Nate shift behind me like they're preparing to attack, but while I might need them to seal the bond, I don't need them for this. I stay still, staring down the alpha with a glare that would make the clan leaders in Seral wilt like dying roses before me. "Remove. Your. Hand." I warn him only once, and luckily for him he listens, reeling back like I've stung him.

"I don't get it," I say to Shade. *"I thought this would be easier. They must know I'm not their mate, so why do they act like I'm the one rejecting them?"*

"The throne of Seral is on the line, and Lady Fate isn't here. You are," Shade replies.

I take note of the alphas' dilated pupils as I take a step back. "You need to get your hands on some of the provisions King Dalton has left around the city. You'll have to fight for them, but that's where you'll find the medication you need, and supplies to keep yourselves comfortable for the remaining nights you're here."

"Supplies?" The bear shifter questions, his gaze hovering on Nate in his small clothes. "I gather you've already found some."

Unease goes through me. "We don't have any more medicine," I say before he gets ideas. "You'll need to obtain more provisions to source your own." I turn to Nate. "Grab them a waterskin and a few parcels of food."

Nate hesitates before disappearing into the building and returning with the supplies. He tosses them to the shifters.

The bear shifter grabs the waterskin and brings it to his mouth, drinking greedily.

"Make it last," I warn him.

He swallows down another mouthful and pulls the waterskin away from his lips, turning his attention to the open doorway behind us. "How do we know you're not lyin' about the medicine? You could have more back there that you're reservin' for your mates as you find them. We're here because of you. The least you could do is share."

My lips flatten. "We have shared. We don't have more medicine, and you're just going to have to trust us on this."

"Trust isn't a word that's used between the different realms," he growls and stares at Nate like he's a traitor. "Or even by some of those within them."

Nate doesn't appear the least bit concerned by his

comment and only grins back. "You should listen to her. There's no point you dyin' for nothing."

The bear shifter bares his teeth, and a gust of wind rushes around the shifters, pulling at their clothes and teasing their hair. "I suggest you leave," Prince Callan says, and there's a dangerous glint in his eyes. "While you still can."

The bear shifter eyes the doorway behind me again, then his hate-filled gaze lands on me. I tense as I mentally prepare myself for a fight. I had hoped I wouldn't have to kill any alphas while in Perstalia, but I get the feeling these shifters aren't going to let this go. My fingers twitch, but I hold still, waiting for the shifters to make the first move.

"Don't do it, buddy," Shade warns as the bear shifter's nostrils flare.

Just as I think they're about to strike, the bear shifter breaks the silence, turning to the alphas beside him. "Let's go," he growls, speaking the words slowly like he's struggling to spit them out.

The other three look just as ready for violence as he is, but when the bear shifter says it again, this time snapping at them, they finally turn and start walking away.

I let out a long breath. Truthfully, I feel a little sorry for the shifters. They thought they were attending a ball, not spending days stumbling around the ruins of Perstalia while their minds betray them. I'm pretty sure Dad is going to make some enemies by performing this little stunt, but then again, Perstalia is neutral ground. I'm guessing the king will argue that their kin could have rescued them at any time. Never mind the fact that no one else knows they're here.

Sighing, I wait until the alphas are out of sight before heading back into the building.

"If the alphas don't get the medicine they need, it's going to get crazy out here soon, whether you find your mates or not," Shade says.

My expression is grim as I wrap up the provisions, tightening the leather ties. In a smooth motion, I heft the pack onto my shoulder just as Nate appears through the doorway. "Allow me," he purrs, holding out his hand and giving me a charming smile that makes my stomach flutter.

I keep a firm hold of the pack. "Yeah, no thanks."

Shade perches on my shoulder. *"Good call not giving it to the thief."*

"What? You don't trust me?" Nate says, pretending that he's offended.

I raise a brow at him. "Would you?"

His grin grows wide. "Fair point, my queen."

"I don't trust those other alphas either," I say, striding through the doorway and onto the street. "We'll find somewhere else to set up camp for a while.

~ Prince Callan ~

She's my Ahalian Touizda. The knowledge haunts me as I keep watch, crouched on the rooftop of a two-story building. We'd walked for an hour and crossed over a bridge before setting up camp in this place. The beast shifters we encountered will likely be able to track us if they are intent on doing so, but I suspect Princess Blake knows that and this is some kind of test for the alphas.

I think about the demon princess resting on the floor below me, and her phantom scent reaches my nose, the sweet honey and spicy cinnamon making my blood pound faster. I grind my teeth as I try to banish the female from my thoughts, but delicious images flash through my mind making my body tighten. I want to taste her, to feel her skin on mine and make her beg for release before I let her come apart in my arms. *Fuck.*

Taking a deep breath, I run a hand through my hair. It wasn't supposed to be like this. As the oldest unbonded prince in the royal Manero line, it was my obligation to attend the ball. To present myself to the princess and keep King Dalton happy. But I hadn't thought the half-blood princess and I would actually be fated. Nor had I anticipated that the demon king would gas us and leave us in an abandoned realm, which was a failure on my part.

My Ahalian Touizda. The truth of the statement vibrates in my bones, but it makes no difference. I can't have her. If I bond with the female nothing would keep me from her side, and I can't let that happen. The promise I made years ago surfaces to the forefront of my mind, a constant reminder of my duty back in Toralyn. No, I can't make Princess Blake mine. Lady Fate made a mistake.

There's a grunt to my left, and I turn my head as Nate climbs onto the roof and settles beside me. He's still wearing the ridiculous outfit that's way too small for his muscled form, and my brows slam down. "What is it, Nine Lives?"

"What's with the hostility, brother?" he replies, baring his teeth. "We're going to be bonded, after all."

I turn my attention back to the street below and crack my knuckles.

Nate stares at the side of my face. "Ah, you're not

still fixated on that promise, are you? Is that why you've been so cold toward our queen?"

"She's not *my* queen," I argue. "She can't be."

"Yes, and that's why you're still here guardin' over her, isn't it?"

"And what about you?" I turn on him. "What's your play, Nine Lives? Because we both know being a royal stuck in a stuffy palace has never been your end goal."

His lips curve into a smile. "Maybe I finally realized that I deserve happiness. I don't know, spendin' the remainder of my days pleasurin' my mate while I enjoy the luxuries of Seral doesn't sound too bad."

I scoff. "You're either fooling yourself or you're fooling her."

His playful smile slips away. "A lot has changed since our last encounter in Toralyn, prince."

"And I dare say not for the better seeing as your head isn't mounted to the Toralyn palace gates," I retort, my jaw clenching.

His expression hardens, his slitted gaze hyperfocused on me. Fangs start to peek from between his lips, but the sound of voices draws my attention to the dark shadows further up the street.

Nate cocks his head, his nostrils flaring. "It's the alphas from earlier. They've found us." He listens for a moment longer, and his features darken.

I draw my sword, careful not to make a sound. "Let me guess, they're not here to make friends?"

"What do you think?" he answers, and his new

clothes shred to pieces as he shifts, fur sprouting over his body, and his muscles rippling as his hands morph into paws.

My lips curve into a wicked smile. "I think it's time to remind the little beasts to have some manners."

~

~ Nate ~

The alphas aren't quiet as they stalk down the street in their non-shifted forms. The bear shifter leads the way, his gaze feral and unfocused, and I stand in the middle of the road, my tail flicking in agitation as I block their path.

Prince Callan drops down beside me and folds his wings behind his back. "I'm going to assume given your current state you don't realize how stupid you are for coming after us," he drawls. "And with that in mind, I'll give you one chance to go back the way you came."

The shifters glare at him and stop where they are.

"We're here for the medicine. We know you have more of it," the bear shifter growls.

"And the demon princess," one of the wolf shifters adds. "She's the reason we're in this mess." The others nod in agreement, fangs already protruding from their mouths as they partially shift.

"Actually, you have the demon king to thank for your current vacation," Prince Callan corrects them. "And there truly is no extra medicine here, so I suggest you turn around and hunker down someplace quiet before someone gets hurt."

"That's easy for you to say. You've got the girl and the medicine," the other wolf shifter snarls. "But what about the rest of us unbonded. We're supposed to just wait around until this little test of her father's is over?"

Prince Callan stares at him like he's an imbecile. "Well, yes."

The shifters all look at each other and laugh.

"C'mon boys, let's see what happens when the princess loses two of her precious mates. They say the bonded feel that pain for the rest of their lives," the bear shifter growls, and his lips form a demented grin. "Maybe she'll change her mind about us when she realizes she's alone again."

One of the wolf shifters lets out a howl, and then the four of them begin to shift, fur sprouting from their skin and their clothes tearing as they surrender to their beasts.

A low growl rumbles in my throat, and I lunge forward before they've transformed completely. In a swift move I tear the head off one of the wolf shifters before he can cry out, and his blood pools in my mouth, dribbling down my chin. The other wolf shifter finishes changing, and he snarls and slavers, his fur bristling as he stares at his fallen comrade. I let out a roar, and the wolf launches toward me. Leaping to the side, I snap my powerful jaws narrowly missing the wolf's neck.

"We did try to warn you," Prince Callan murmurs as he stalks casually forward, meeting the giant reptilian shifter head on. The beast has a thick body with spines running down his curved back, and an elongated snout containing rows of razor-sharp teeth. The prince grins as he confuses the shifter with his wind power and runs his sword into its side. The creature lets out a pained clicking sound and flicks his head, his teeth scraping on Prince Callan's metal breastplate. Grunting comes from the right, and the bear shifter runs at the prince. Before the beast can barrel into him, Prince Callan lifts his hand and blows the bear back with his power.

I turn my attention to the wolf who's watching me. His head is lowered, his yellow eyes alert and calculating. I pace, moving as he does, my tail flicking back and forth. It isn't my first time against wolves, so when the beast lunges forward, I do the same. We clash in the air, and my paw smashes against the wolf's face, leaving deep claw marks over his eye. He whines and twists as he tries to clamp his teeth onto my shoulder, but all he's done is leave himself open, and my jaws lock onto his head. I bare down, crushing bone until he falls limp in my hold.

The thrill of the kill rushes through me, and I growl as I toss his body to the side. To my right, the reptilian shifter is dead on the ground, and Prince Callan battles the bear shifter, using his wind power to force the creature toward the building at his back. I move closer, drawn by my bloodlust and the adrenaline pumping through my veins.

The bear growls, lifting his head and showing his fangs as he fights against the wind and swipes at Prince Callan. The prince side steps, avoiding the hit, and I jog to the bear's left side, ready to attack the beast while he's distracted.

The bear grunts and swipes at Prince Callan again, his eyes tearing from the swirling wind. Seeing my opening, I lunge forward. I'm about to close my jaws onto the creature's neck when the bear is lifted a few feet into the air. My teeth snap at empty air, and I glare at Prince Callan who's now flapping his wings, hovering in the air as well.

He smirks at me. "Oh, did I not mention that this one's mine? You weren't expecting me to let you have more kills than me now, were you?"

I snarl at him, and pace agitated as he makes quick work of the flailing bear shifter. Within a matter of moments, the bear's head thuds to the ground near my paws, crimson blood running into the cracks between the stones. The wind swirling around the creature's suspended body stops, and the rest of the beast falls to the street. Prince Callan grins wickedly, his sword slick with blood as he flaps his wings, landing beside the fallen alpha. "Without the medicine, they were so weak it wasn't a fair fight," Prince Callan comments, then he smiles. "Not that the outcome would have been any different."

ELEVEN

~ Princess Blake ~

"I was starting to think you weren't going to come," Kai says as he lifts from the dining room chair, looking exactly the same in my dream as I remember him. He's dressed in a crisp white shirt with a black silk tie, and his dark hair has been slicked away from his face. He takes in my appearance as I approach, his gaze roving over the claw marks cut deep into my leathers as the guards close the doors behind me.

Concern enters Kai's gaze. "Then again, maybe I should be grateful you made it at all?"

The blood on my face cracks as my lips quirk upward, and I gesture to the silver cloches on the table. "You could have eaten. Honestly, I didn't expect you to still be here." This is the third night Kai has visited the palace, and I'm *not sure why he keeps coming. We both know we're not mates. His scent is so weak that when I'm close to him, I can hardly smell anything at all, and there's no burning desire when we're near one another. Nothing that makes me desperate to pull him to me and lose myself in his touch. At this point, I can only guess he's as lonely as I am, and he's still hoping that we're both wrong about us not being fated. Either way, I decide that tonight it doesn't matter.*

It's been nights since I won the king's tournament, and yet, I just had to face another trial for my father. Retrieve an item he left in the shadow realm. That was the goal. I shudder, remembering the way the shadow beings hunted me as I moved swiftly through the gray landscape. Their claws reached for me, their shadowy teeth tearing through my flesh though I never felt the pain. Only the fear. It wasn't until I'd retrieved the king's dagger from a group of wraiths, and I was back in Seral with the blade secure in my grasp, that I had noticed the blood coating my body. The cuts on my cheeks, arms, and legs healed quickly, but the blood remains, a visual display of my weakness.

I remember my father's approving smile as I had handed him the dagger not long after. He'd glanced at the blade, then tossed it onto his desk like it was of no consequence. I didn't wait to hear whatever philosophical message he wanted to impart. Truthfully, I'm not sure if he had one. Instead, I had made my way straight to the dining hall, the memory of the shadow beings still haunting me, and my body ice cold, as if I'd been in the snowy mountains in Rostof.

No, tonight Kai is just what I need.

*"What could be better than dining with the princess?"
he says with a seductive smile, and I walk straight to him,
not bothering with the food. He's not my mate, but for all I
know, I might not have any mates out there. For now, he's
the next best thing.*

*"Better than dining? I can think of a few things," I say
as I stop beside him and yank on his tie, bringing his lips to
mine. He's stunned for a moment, but then he leans in, his
hands winding around my waist as he deepens the kiss. His
tongue dips into my mouth, sweeping over mine, and I grip
onto his broad shoulders. Warmth goes through me as I kiss
him, my body responding, but there's no spark. Either way,
it's enough for now.*

*He breaks the kiss just long enough to speak. "When
you'd agreed to another dinner, I'd hoped, but I hadn't
thought this is what you had in mind," he murmurs.*

*"Shut up," I breathe, desperate to forget. For two
seconds, I need control. And I need to feel. I need to chase
away the ice that's hardened my veins and dulled my fire.*

*He steps away from his chair and pivots me toward the
table, kissing me harder. I can tell it's the same for him. The
spark he's looking for just isn't there, but he doesn't pull
away, almost as if he needs this as much as I do.*

*Reaching up, I rip off his shirt revealing an expanse of
hardened muscle, and he removes my clothes, leaving them
in pieces on the floor. My nipples pucker as they're exposed
to the cool air, and his eyes darken as he drinks me in.*

*"So beautiful," he rasps low and deep, and the words
make my stomach clench. He kisses me again and moves
between my thighs, pressing against me.*

I want to curse Lady Fate. Being with Kai would be easy. But my life is never easy.

His dark gaze drops to my face, and I think I see a flicker of blue in his eyes, but I blink and it's gone. "You sure you want this, your highness?"

I bristle at the formality of his words. "If I didn't, you wouldn't be between my legs right now," I answer sweetly.

He chuckles and moves back just enough to remove his pants. Then his arms hook under my knees, and he teases me with the tip of his cock. He waits until I'm writhing and panting, and then with a hard thrust he's inside me. I gasp as he pushes deep, not holding back, and taking me just like I want him to. The wood groans and I moan, my back arching off the polished table.

"Harder," I command, and he slams into me with more force, making the plates rattle and bounce near my head.

"I take it you've had a rough night?" he manages between grunts.

My body heats even more, and I suck in a sharp breath as he hits a delicious spot deep inside me. He might not be my mate, but he knows what he's doing, and pleasure winds through my body. "The worst," I manage.

There's another flicker of concern in his gaze, but it's gone quickly, like he knows the last thing I need right now is his pity. He fucks me harder and the world fades away, my mind focusing on the moment and the pleasure. I know it won't last, but it's enough that my bones thaw, and the chill of the shadow realm starts to disappear. My body continues to heat, and I feel lighter than I have in a long time.

I look up at him. Sweat drips down Kai's temple, trailing down past his eyes, and his gaze searches my face. I don't know what he's looking for, but his expression slackens in surprise before he smiles, his lush lips twisting into a smirk. "I've got you, princess," he drawls.

My heart flutters. Demons don't talk to me like this. Not ever. They're usually either falling over themselves to follow my commands or shouting slurs at me when I'm facing them in combat.

But Kai's speaking as if we're…more than friends. I close my eyes as my throat tightens. It's a mistake doing this right after my latest trial, but I can't bring myself to regret it. Kai quickens his thrusts, and I cry out, my nails digging into the wooden table. I need this. Right now, I need him. A surge of power goes through me as I near my release, the magic building and making my body tingle. What? I've been with males before, but it's never been like this. Every nerve comes alive, sizzling with power, but just as I'm about to tip over the edge, a strange chill cuts through me, my blood turning to ice like I'm back in the shadow realm. The feeling is gone within seconds, but the rush of power starts to fade, and I snap my eyes open. Floral marks illuminate my skin, a pattern of golden tattoos shining in the dim light, but they disappear quickly until my skin is smooth and bare again.

"Did you feel that?" I gasp, but Kai doesn't answer. With jerky movements, he releases my legs and steps away from me.

I lift my gaze to his face. "Kai, I—" I don't finish, and my eyes shoot wide. Kai's mouth gapes open like he's struggling for air, and no sound is coming out. He takes another step away from me, his nails digging into his skin as he claws at his neck as if he's trying to free himself from something.

"Kai?" my voice wobbles as I jump up from the table. "What is it?"

The demon drops to the floor, jerking and writhing, and before I can reach him, he stills, his mouth open in a silent scream. And then he vanishes.

What the fuck? Kai? *My heart lurches, and I crouch to where I'd last seen him, swiping my hands through the empty air. I know he's dead, but usually when a soul is sent to the shadow realm, the body remains. Unlike me, he's not sneaking in the back door of the realm. No, he's walked through the front gates.*

I swallow hard, staring at the smooth skin of my arm, right where the marks had been moments ago. Somehow, I caused this, and guilt rises in me when I remember his words: I've got you, princess. *I'd wanted him to help me banish the memories of the shadow realm, and now I've taken everything from him. Unlike me, he'll never find his way back.*

The dream changes, and I find myself outside the forbidden door in the underground vault. Power pulses from within, and an ancient voice whispers in my ear, as soft as a caress though I can't make out the words. I take a step closer to the door and to whatever lies within, and invisible fingers rake over my skin, the energy making my body vibrate. I still can't make out the whispers, but the words become more frequent, like the power is frantic for me to move closer. Dread pools in my stomach, but for some reason it feels right to keep moving toward the door. I take another step. One more and the scanner will know that I'm there. My right foot lifts into the air, but before I step forward, I smell it.

The scent of bitter chocolate fills my senses, warm and creamy, and sweet. It coats my tongue, and the invisible fingers of power loosen their grip on my shoulders.

⁓

I gasp, my eyes shooting open as Shade squawks, startling from where she'd been perched on the end of a decayed bookcase. It's the first time I've slept that deeply in months, maybe even years, and my mind is still a mess as I peer up at where Nate and Prince Callan are standing.

Blood coats Nate's chin and fingers, and Prince Callan's breast plate is covered in scratch marks. By my legs, I peer down at the objects that woke me. The severed heads of four alpha shifters are clumped together, blood pooling around them as the males stare silently ahead. *What the fuck?*

Shade ruffles her feathers and makes a disgusted noise in my mind. *"Can you ask your mates to warn us next time before they go tossing heads around?"*

I blink, lifting my gaze to where Nate is smirking, and Prince Callan has a self-satisfied smile on his face.

"What is this?" I ask, though I instantly recognize

the four alphas we encountered not too long ago. *Dammit. Why didn't they stay away?*

"Our friends from earlier tracked us here. They were convinced we were hiding more medicine," Prince Callan explains.

I nod, knowing full well what he really means. That the shifters came looking for something we didn't have, and they were willing to spill blood to get it.

"I took down the wolves," Nate grins like he's proud of himself. "Would have taken the bear, too, if the prince hadn't gotten in my way."

Even though they've reverted to their non-shifted forms, the bear shifter's head is the biggest of the four, and I can't stop staring at the lifeless expression on his face. Seeing the alphas like this shouldn't bother me, but memories of the shadow realm and of Kai make me queasy. "Okay," I say slowly, trying to focus on the present. "But none of this explains why their heads are *here*."

Both of my mates are silent for a moment, and Prince Callan looks genuinely confused. "Oh, would you rather their fingers?" he says like he's figured me out. "Because that can be arranged."

I make a face. "What? No."

"*Wow, Blake. Your mates are even more fucked up than you are,*" Shade comments on the verge of laughter.

I stare at the archangel expecting him to crack a smile, but he only looks at me expectantly like he's waiting for me to tell him what color roses I like. Only, we're discussing body parts, and carrying around someone's decaying limb just sounds like a pointless activity. I resist the urge to rub the bridge of my nose. "You know what, good job," I say as I stand, and I partly mean it because if the alphas were here to kill us, they got what they deserved. "But next time you can just tell me what happened. I don't need the visual aid."

Nate shrugs. "Where's the fun in that?"

I decide I'm not even going to try to tackle that question.

"As you wish, princess," Prince Callan drawls.

"And can you please put some clothes on," I say to Nate as I struggle not to stare at his raging erection. I'm not sure if it's because he enjoyed killing, or because of me, but I can't focus with that thing staring at me.

Nate grins, and I think he's going to say something stupid, but he only turns and finds the leather satchel. Rummaging around in the contents, he pulls out a black t-shirt and pants. It's the only pair of clothing left. When he pulls the shirt on, it doesn't even reach below his belly button, and the pants tear at the seams, somehow only just managing to stay together.

"Better?" he says, smirking at me.

I stifle my smile. "It'll do."

TWELVE

~ Princess Blake ~

More alphas find us in the hours that follow, likely drawn by the scent of blood, but that suits me just fine. This place is getting to everyone, and the sooner I find my mates before they've all lost their minds the better things will go for me. But one after the other, I discover that none of them are mine. Thankfully, these alphas actually heed my advice and leave to find some place to hunker down. Or at least, I hope they do.

We're walking down a street that has the trunk of a dead oak in the middle of the aged cobblestones, when I see flashes of movement up ahead.

Nate narrows his gaze on the objects in the

distance. "It's a group of archangels. They look a little rough."

"Archangels?" I turn to Prince Callan who's striding behind us, but he keeps staring ahead, his expression harder than usual.

It's not until we're closer that I make out a dozen archangels on the street. Many of them are wet, their sodden wings spread on the ground as they lay on the cobblestones, blood seeping from wounds on their bodies. A few of them are pacing, mumbling under their breath, and one is cradling his knees to his chest as he rocks against a wall, shouting curses at someone I can't see.

"Well, these guys all look...chipper," Shade comments sarcastically. *"I didn't know it just rained?"*

"It didn't," I confirm, frowning at the archangels' wet clothes and turning my attention to a nearby building. A water symbol is etched into the stone above the door, curly waves surrounded by a thick circle.

"Careful. These alphas look like they're one word away from breakin'," Nate warns. "Guessin' they didn't get their hands on any medicine."

"I don't think it's because of a lack of trying," I comment, turning my attention back to the alphas who all look like they've just battled something horrible.

One of the pacing archangels lifts his head, and I instantly recognize the male who was knocked over by the giant in the ballroom. His bronze wings have lost some of their color, and the alpha's face is uncharacteristically pale, but otherwise he appears to be whole.

"Our prince?" the archangel says tentatively like his eyes have tricked him before, and he's not sure whether to believe what he's seeing.

Prince Callan strolls past Nate and me to greet him. "Theon. I must say, you've looked better."

"Haven't we all," Theon replies with a weak grin. His gaze slides from Prince Callan to me, and his brows rise. "It seems you've fared better."

"I don't know if he would agree," Nate grins.

Theon finally looks at the shifter, and his top lip curls in distaste. "Nine Lives? Of course, you'd survive this place."

Nate laughs like he's just been given a compliment.

"Speaking of surviving," I say, stepping up to Prince Callan's side. "What's happened here?" Now that I'm closer, I pick up Theon's scent. He doesn't smell unpleasant, but nothing sparks in me at our close proximity. He must feel the same way, because he stares at me for a long moment, and then there's only acceptance in his gaze.

"It's a bathhouse," he replies, gesturing to the building with the water symbol. "We figured there might be provisions here, but the water..." His expression shutters, and he clears his throat. "None of us have found the medicine, and Saphis is among those who never emerged from the bath."

"Who's Saphis?" I ask.

Prince Callan lets out a breath through his nose. "So that's why he hasn't been able to heal any of you."

"Yes," Theon confirms, his expression darkening.

I recall the archangel who had healed the giant back in the ballroom. "And you say he's still in the water? Is there any chance—"

My words trail off when Theon shakes his head. "I tried to go after him. Many of us did, and we're lucky any of us were able to get out alive."

"Okay." I nod as I process what he's told me. "So, what's in there?"

Theon stares at me blankly.

"In the water," I clarify. "It'd help if we knew what we were dealing with."

Fear enters Theon's gaze, and he starts mumbling about rainbows in the water. I have no idea whether it's the sickness messing with his mind, but when he still doesn't say anything that makes sense for a while after, I turn and start striding toward the bathhouse.

Prince Callan is quick to step into my path. "What are you doing?"

"I'm going to get the medicine," I say, giving him an unimpressed look and gesturing to the archangels. "They clearly need it, and maybe, I'll find out what happened to your friend, Syphilis."

"Saphis," Prince Callan corrects as Nate snorts, trying to contain his laughter.

I wave my hand dismissively. "Oh right, *Saphis.*"

"If anyone's going in there, it'll be me," Prince

Callan says. "This is my responsibility. You and Nine Lives can stay out here."

My lips form a thin line, and both Shade and I stare at him like he's delusional. Because he is.

Nate bumps the prince on his way to the bathhouse. "Like fuck am I stayin' out here with these guys. Most of them hate me, and they might start usin' their powers while in their current state. Unless you want me killing them all, I'm takin' my chances with the haunted bath."

Prince Callan looks like he wants to argue, but I follow after the shifter before he can utter a word. The bathhouse is a tall rectangular structure, and I pull out my sword as Nate leads the way through the entrance archway and down a stone corridor. The air cools, and we step into a cavernous room that contains a large bath. The pool of water almost spans the entire width of the space, but there's just enough room to walk along the edges and past the thick concrete pillars that are evenly placed to act as supports for the structure. A massive panel of frosted glass forms the ceiling above the bath, and dappled sunlight streams onto the still water, illuminating the room. I'm still covered in slime from our fight with the demon bugs, and if I wasn't convinced that something terrible was in there, I would have enjoyed the thought of having a bath. I scan the area expecting to find blood stains and obvious signs of a struggle, but there's nothing to suggest any archangels have even been here.

Paintings cover the walls of the bathhouse,

depicting pictures of trees and rivers, and showing how everything in Perstalia is connected like in the mural I saw when I first arrived. I run my hand over the cracked paint that's closest to me and wipe off a layer of dust, while keeping the bath in my peripheral. Just like with the mural, the small gems embedded in the stone gleam and sparkle as soon as the dust is cleared away.

"How can it be full?" Prince Callan mutters. "I thought Perstalia doesn't have any water?"

I turn my attention back to the bath. "It doesn't," I reply, then add. "Well, it didn't."

Nate steps right up to the edge of the water and peers in. "So, what do you think we're dealing with here?"

"Could be any number of things," I reply. "There are at least a dozen water creatures in Seral, and all of them are nasty. I almost died once when I was little, when Dad told me to practice swimming in the river just outside the city. Of course, it was another character-building exercise, and he didn't mention that the river was home to a Derois. I think it was mostly luck that I survived, because the creature wasn't that hungry that night."

Both Prince Callan and Nate stare at me like I've grown another head.

I stare back at them. "What?"

Nate shakes his head. "Your relationship with your father is fucked up, gorgeous. For the first time, I'm honestly glad I never knew my parents."

I blink and it takes me a moment to realize what he's said. "Wait, you're an orphan?"

He doesn't answer, but instead he strips off his clothes and tosses them against the wall. And then his body is changing, fur bursting from his skin as he grows in size. I'll never get used to seeing it, and I'm still staring when the giant cat pads up beside me, his massive paws nearly silent on the stone.

I sheath my sword and lean down, picking up a pebble that's sitting near my boot. I throw the smooth rock into the air and catch it, testing the weight of it in my hand, then I toss it across the water. The pebble skims along the surface for three jumps before sinking in. I brace as I wait for some beast to explode from the water, but the bathhouse remains quiet.

Nate's tail flicks as he crouches at the edge of the bath, his nose almost touching the water.

Prince Callan strolls casually behind me, and I'm about to pick up another stone when Nate lets out a howl and there's a loud splash. I whip my head to the side only to find Prince Callan is standing in Nate's place, a wicked smirk on his face.

"What happened to it being *your* responsibility?" I ask the grinning archangel.

He only shrugs. "It *is* my responsibility, and Nine Lives is being useful for once, and he's helping me to figure out what's in there."

I pivot toward the water, my muscles tensing as I prepare myself to dive in and save my mate, but to my surprise, Nate isn't thrashing around like I expected.

He swims with powerful strokes, keeping his head above the surface and acting like he's enjoying himself. He's in the middle of the pool when lights burst to life in the water around him, a rainbow of colors flickering on like lights that have been turned on.

Huh. So Theon wasn't entirely crazy. I lean closer, and my eyes widen when I make out the shapes of small fish that are no longer than my hands. The majority of their bodies are a translucent gray, their skeletons visible through their flesh, but light shines from their midsections and fins, the colorful glow mesmerizing.

"Shade, have you seen anything like that?"

"They almost look like goldfish," she replies, sounding just as awed as I am. *"Very colorful and slightly freaky goldfish."*

"Well, that's not exactly what I was expecting," Prince Callan mutters.

"The king wouldn't have put them here unless they were dangerous," I comment, though it's hard for me to imagine how these fish could be a threat. I've never heard of glowing fish in Seral.

Prince Callan nods, and I slide off my boots leaving them by the side of the pool.

"Either that, or they're not the threat and there's something else in there," I amend as Nate swims around like he's not in a hurry to get out of the water.

"I thought cats hate water," Shade says like she's fascinated.

"I guess not all of them," I say, smiling at the jaguar. *"But unless you want to come for a dip, you might want to find somewhere safe to wait."*

I don't need to tell Shade again. She flaps from my shoulder and hops down onto the stone floor, standing as far from the bath as she can. *"Don't make me worry, Blake,"* she calls in my head, repeating something she often said when I'd have to face one of Dad's challenges alone. *"Get in and get out."*

"In and out," I agree. I'm about to strip off my clothes when Prince Callan starts unfastening the buckles at his sides, and he lifts his chest plate armor up over his head.

I rest a hand on my hip. "What makes you think you're—" A sharp cry pierces the air, cutting me off, and I turn as Nate hisses and growls, thrashing in the water.

The fish are swimming in a circular motion as they surround him, and every time one of them brushes by him, he cries out in agony.

Panic slices through me. I rationalize that it's because if I lose any of my mates, I won't be able to seal the bond with my guys and unlock my power, but in that moment, I'm not thinking about that. All I see is my mate, and he's in trouble.

"Get out of the water," I shout at Nate like he isn't already trying to paddle closer to the edge of the bath. The fish block his way, a wall of glowing lights constantly zapping him. Growling, Nate closes his fangs around a fish and hisses in pain as the creature's blood dribbles down his chin, burning his skin like acid.

Prince Callan curses, and I don't give myself time to think. Bringing my hands together above my head, I suck in a deep breath and dive into the water.

I think I hear a shout behind me, but the sound is muffled as the cool water swallows me, bubbles clouding around my face. There's an explosion of neon color, and soon I'm surrounded by little glowing fish that are circling my position. There must be hundreds of them in the bath, and the moment one of them touches my arm, a jolt of electricity travels up my bones, making my teeth chatter and setting my nerves on fire. It's not even the pain that's the worst part. Every time they touch me it's as if some of my energy is draining away, like they're making me weaker.

I swim back up to the surface, my head bursting above the water, and my gaze locks onto Nate's position. He's not far from me, his body covered in wounds, and his spotted fur is burned away in patches to reveal raw flesh. He growls when he sees me and stops trying to get to the edge of the pool, angling in my direction instead.

"No!" I yell, annoyed that he's not solely focused on escaping. My body tingles, already hard at work healing me every time another fish zaps my skin, but shifters don't heal like demons do, and I'm surprised Nate has lasted this long.

"Get your ass over here, Nine Lives," Prince Callan shouts from where he's leaning over the edge of the bath, waiting to grab the giant cat out of the water. "She can handle it in there, but you're not looking so good."

Nate growls in response and reluctantly turns back to Prince Callan. He pushes forward with his massive paws, and I catch up to him in a few strokes. There's a mass of fish between us and the edge of the pool like the fish are creating a wall with their bodies, and I grit my teeth as I move in front of Nate, swimming into them to try and clear a path for the shifter. The acid blood in the water makes my skin sizzle, and my head spins as I fight against the pain and unnatural exhaustion, but I keep going. I can't lose my mate.

"You're almost there!" Shade squawks at me, her voice panicked, and I don't have the energy to respond. The zapping gets worse like the fish are desperate to keep us there, but I snarl as I push them away with my hands, my fingers igniting with pain as I clear the last part of the way.

Prince Callan's hand grips onto my leather vest, but I bat him away.

"Grab Nate!" I yell.

The prince's gaze is hard and reluctant, but when I move out of the way to let Nate through, he doesn't hesitate to grip the back of the jaguar's neck and start pulling. Nate hisses, showing his fangs, but he doesn't try to harm the prince as the pair of them work together, and Nate lifts his paws onto the edge, helping haul his massive body out of the water.

Relief floods my system at the sight of Nate safely

out of the bath, but the fish continue to zap me, draining my energy away.

"Get out of there, Blake," Shade pleads, hopping closer to the edge of the water. *"I know you want to help, but you need to get out."*

She's barely finished speaking when ice cold fingers wrap around my right ankle. I freeze as despair sinks into my skin, and my heart begins to pound faster.

Prince Callan's gaze meets mine as he reaches for me, but it's already too late. With one hard yank, the hand pulls me under.

Memories flash before my eyes, and suddenly I'm eight again, swimming in the lake outside Seral City. When the king told me to practice my swimming, I'd been so determined to show him how far I could manage without stopping. The current pushed against me, pulling at my gangly limbs, but I forced myself to continue through the frigid water. I'd barely done ten strokes when he'd pulled me under. The creature. The monster in the water.

I'd fought against him that day, thrashing in the lake to try and get him to release his grip, but this time I don't bother. I'm still as I let the creature pull me under, dragging me down into the dark water far beneath me.

The bath is impossibly deep, and I soon realize

there is no bottom. Or at least, not one I can see. Whatever this place is, it isn't just a bath, and I'm not sure if it's because Dad changed it, or if it was always this way. I try to send a message to Shade, but it's like I can't reach her. As if something is blocking our connection.

My lungs burn the longer I'm submerged, small bubbles slipping past my lips. I'm a demon, an immortal, but that doesn't mean I can't drown. It just means I come back to life after a short while. I could be trapped in an endless cycle of drowning if the creature kept me down here. *Fuck.* I knew the fish couldn't be all Dad had in store. As hard and painful as they were, they still weren't enough of a challenge. Not for the demon king. They were only a distraction from the real threat.

I feel impossibly empty as I continue to be pulled downward, the despair winding through my body like a poison as the bony hand wrapped around my ankle continues to hold tight, never letting go. I don't want to look at him, don't want to see one of the many faces that haunt my nightmares, but I force myself to keep my eyes open. My vision adjusts to the darkness, the fish far above us and not following us down, and I don't let myself react when I make out his massive, twisted limbs and bulging black eyes. He's easily three times my size, with gills along his scaled neck, and fangs that protrude in all directions. Some say he's a creature from the spirit realm that escaped into Seral. Others say he's a mutilation born from the deepest parts of the river. All I know is, he's in my way.

"Princess of death," he hisses in my mind with an ancient voice that makes the back of my neck prickle. *"Oh, how I've waited for you."*

"You shouldn't have," I reply sarcastically. *"I'm sure you can find much better."*

His laughter in my head should be enough to make my courage wither, but I grit my teeth. He's just another monster, and I won't let him have me.

He stops swimming and comes up beside me, his slimy tongue trailing up my cheek. I cringe, but I don't react.

"Still just as delicious, and not as bland as the demons," he hisses in appreciation. *"When I let you go as a child, I knew one day you'd be mine. And here you are, my bride. Oh, how you'll suffer, and I'll get to watch it all. When the king came to me with a bargain, I was dubious, but the moment he mentioned your hand in return for my services in Perstalia, I could no longer refuse."*

My hand? So that's how Dad persuaded him to come here. Unfortunately for the monster, he doesn't realize that bargain was likely a lie like many things that spill from the king's mouth. I resist the urge to grab out my dagger and stab the monster in the side. From what I gather, he wants me to stay in the watery depths with him, in a constant state of drowning and coming back for small snippets. I still remember him saying something about us having monster babies all those years ago, and just the thought of it makes my stomach roil. If it weren't for my angel blood igniting his interest when I was a child, I might not have survived our last encounter, but now the attention it's getting me is a pain in my ass.

"The only one who's going to suffer will be you," I reply sweetly, responding to the monster's earlier comment.

He laughs again, and the sound is like a gurgling, drowning noise in my head. *"Such spirit. I'm going to miss your quick tongue when I've broken you."*

He continues pulling me downward, and my lungs burn in protest at the lack of air. *Fuck.* I've been down for too long. I think about holding on longer, but it's better if I let it happen now before I've reached his lair. I don't fight it as the water floods into my mouth, my body jerking as I drown. And then I'm no longer in Perstalia.

Seconds. That's all it is. Seconds when I'm suspended in the shadow realm, walking with the true dead, and then I'm back in the water, my heart beating rapidly with life.

We've reached some kind of underwater cave, and he pulls me past the bodies of four archangels. Three of them are headless, their souls walking the shadow realm, but the fourth is in some kind of air bubble, his body paralyzed. I recognize Saphis from the ballroom, though his skin is deathly pale.

Not far from the angels is a small silver chest. *The provisions.*

"Princess of death," the monster hisses in my head. *"Yes, yes. I'll keep you always. But first, the cage."* Ahead is

a box consisting of rusted, thick metal bars on all sides. It's only just big enough for me, and I can't let him put me in there.

Peering back, I eye the bubble around Saphis's head. If I can get to it, I can breathe. The monster pulls me closer to the opening in the cage, and I can't wait any longer. My lungs burn as I pull out my dagger, and I keep my grip tight on the hilt as I stab into the monster's gills. Even with my strength, I couldn't pierce his scales, but my blade punctures through the thin openings, and he screeches a high-pitched wail that vibrates through the water.

I don't waste time. Leaving the dagger embedded, I swim to Saphis, my lips breaking into the bubble of air just in time. I gasp, sucking in a breath, and pivot, angling toward the chest of provisions. I yank on the lid. If I can open it, there must be weapons in there. Dad would have prepared for this, and I can only guess he's put something in there that can defeat the monster. The lid doesn't budge, and I pull harder, wedging my fingers under the rim. *Fuck. Has this been sealed by magic? Fuck, it won't—* The lid finally gives way, and I push it open, frantically searching the contents. *Weapon. There must be a weapon.* I glimpse parcels of food and flasks of water. There's a small selection of daggers, but... My heart sinks. There's nothing else here. Aside from the ordinary blades, there's no weapon that would give me an advantage against the lake creature. My fingers tremble, and I pull out the sword at my side.

"My violent little bride," the monster's voice sounds in my head, and I turn to see he's removed the dagger, and his skin has already healed. *The Unkillable.* That's what the demons in Seral call the monster. Even if you sever his head, he doesn't die, and is said to grow another.

My heart pounds. I try moving away, but I can't outswim him, and soon his clawed hands are on me again dragging me down. I kick a leg free and slam it into his face, then I lash out with my sword, but he grabs me, restraining my limbs with his four arms.

"Such excitement. Have I ever had such excitement?" he hisses. I struggle, but he pulls me closer to the cage again.

No. No. No!

The bars draw closer, and I snarl, but I can't break free from his iron grip. So close. Just as he's about to push me inside, bubbles trail past my face, and a large bubble of air envelopes the monster's head. He screeches and thrashes, releasing me as he tries to get away from it.

But the bubble follows him, the air making him suffocate. I turn to see Prince Callan not far away in the water, his expression serious as he concentrates, controlling the air bubble, while another bubble surrounds his own face. He sends one in my direction, and I cough and wheeze as I suck in the air and swim straight for the chest of provisions, my relief near crippling.

I scoop up the chest with one hand, and rush over

to Saphis. Seaweed is wrapped around his ankles and anchoring him, but I sever them with my blade and use my other arm to lift the archangel, slowly making my way upward.

Prince Callan moves after me as I travel past him, and he hooks one hand under Saphis's other arm as he helps me carry the paralyzed archangel to the surface.

"Princess!" The anguished cry of the monster makes my blood turn to ice. *"You will not leave me again!"*

I feel the monster's magic as it implodes in the water, spreading outward, and a rush of despair stronger than anything I've felt slams into me making my limbs weak. The emotion sucks away my energy, weighing me down, and clouding my mind. I struggle to remember what I'm doing, or even where I am, and I see the same confusion on Prince Callan's face. His air magic wavers, the bubbles disappearing from around our faces and from the monster.

The creature swims after us shooting in our direction, and we remain still in the water, the darkness closing in on me, and suddenly I'm eight again. Eight and full of fear as the world closes off to me. Eight and lost in the unknown. The despair weighs on me like a stone pulling me deeper into the darkness. Prince Callan's free hand floats in the water, and his fingers brush across my cheek.

The only thing is, this time I'm not alone. And perhaps, I never was, even all those years ago.

"This will be your life for eternity, my dearest, and

you'll never see the light again," the monster rages in my head as he draws closer, and my mind clears just enough to register what he's said.

The light. I hold on, fighting against the burning in my lungs. *He hates the light!* Closing my eyes, I focus my power. The monster might be unkillable, but we don't need to kill him to escape. We only need a distraction. There aren't any crows in Perstalia, not besides Shade, and I haven't connected with any other beings. I never believed it was possible, but I focus my mind, hoping. I can feel the monster coming closer. Feel the movement in the water.

Please. Please hear my call. I hadn't thought to try it before, but now my power reaches out. Searching. Hoping. Commanding. Just as my lungs feel as though they're about to burst. Just as the monster is about to grab me, the connection snaps into place. It feels different, the power swirling through me, my veins a mix of ice and fire, but the chatter of the little fish floods my mind, *"Lost. We're lost."* I don't have time to try and understand what they're talking about. I send a single thought, one command to them: *"Show the monster how bright you can shine."*

The monster wraps his fingers painfully around my thigh, but he recoils as hundreds of neon colors spiral down from above. The fish move around me, Prince Callan, and Saphis, never touching us, and they circle the monster, sliding close and zapping his scales.

He screeches in anger, the water amplifying his cry

of rage and making my ears bleed. *"Too bright!"* he yells.

The distraction is enough. His power wavers, the crippling despair easing, and Prince Callan shakes his head as his mind clears. Using his power, he pulls down more air bubbles from above, and we escape upward together. With powerful strokes, we swim until we break the surface, and then Nate's hands are on us, pulling us from the water.

CHAPTER

THIRTEEN

~ Princess Blake ~

I suck in air greedily as I flop on to the cold stone, and the chest of provisions drops beside me. I'm still gasping as I send a message to the fish. *Thank you. You can leave him alone now.* The monster can't get to us now that we're out of the water, and I hope he hasn't killed too many of the fish. Dozens of voices reply in my head, *"Still lost. Forever lost."* I don't know what it means, but before I can question them, the swell of power in my chest fades and our connection is cut off.

Lifting my head, I peer at where Prince Callan has collapsed nearby, his golden lips paler than usual and his hair plastered to his head.

"You all right, gorgeous?" Nate asks, crouching

over me with concern etched into his features. Burn marks still cover his body, the wounds only just starting to heal, but he's wearing his clothes again, and he doesn't look nearly as bad as I thought he would. "You were down there for a long time."

"I'm okay," I wheeze.

A hint of guilt touches his eyes. "I'd have jumped in after you if I'd thought I would be much use down there."

My lips part. I'm not sure what to respond to that, but I'm distracted when Shade appears above me, her beady eyes staring into mine. *"Girl, what the hell happened? I nearly just died of a heart attack!"* She paces on my chest. *"First, I couldn't connect with you, and then the prince disappeared as well, and neither of you came back—"*

"Everything is fine," I say, though the words don't exactly sound truthful, even to my own ears. I'd always known that one day I might have to face the lake monster again, and I'd thought I would be more prepared, but he nearly had me. I shudder, and Shade's feathered face moves closer to mine.

"Liar!" she accuses. *"You're not okay. Are you going to tell me what happened down there?"*

Sitting up, I bring her close, crushing her against me. I tell myself the hug is for her, but the truth is I need it, too. *"You're right, I'm not really okay. But I will be."* She quiets as she leans against me, and my blood warms just a little.

"Wake up, dammit," Prince Callan growls as he

checks on Saphis. He lifts the archangel onto his side, rubbing the male's back, and after a long moment, Saphis starts to cough and wretch, vomiting up water. Relief softens Prince Callan's eyes, and his gaze meets mine for a heartbeat before he turns his attention back to the archangel.

"Where am I?" Saphis croaks, his skin still deathly pale. "The creature. The others?"

Prince Callan gives him a somber look. "You're alive. That's all that matters."

Saphis's expression droops, but slowly, the color returns to his cheeks, and he lets out a long breath that makes his chest sag.

Letting go of Shade, I rise to my feet, and Nate helps to steady me when my head spins. For a moment, I swear I can smell the faintest trace of chocolate. Which is weird, but I shake it off and pick up the chest of provisions.

"So," I say with a smile. "Shall we get these supplies to your guys?"

Prince Callan's gaze roves over me, and if I didn't know better, I would think he was searching for wounds. Eventually, he lifts his eyes back to my face and nods, then he pulls on his armor. "They'll be waiting."

My sodden wings are too heavy for me to lift, so I let them trail behind me as I stride toward the corridor that leads outside. Shade flies up to my shoulder, and I hear the others following behind.

We're almost at the front door when Shade calls out, *"Blake."*

I pause, peering in the direction that she's looking. Just behind me, a long black feather sits in a puddle of water on the stones. I hear it's not uncommon for angels to lose feathers, but it's the first one I've ever lost, and I frown. *"Well, that's new."* Ignoring the feather, I turn forward again and keep walking.

I'm not sure if it's because of the encounter with the water monster, but the moment we're on the street again, that familiar sensation of being watched makes my skin crawl. I only have two daggers left after losing blades in the water, but I'm tempted to grab one of them out when Prince Callan moves to my side, distracting me.

"There had better actually be medicine in there," he mutters, his eyes locked on the chest I'm cradling, and I give him a reassuring smile as I place the chest down and pry open the lid.

"Plenty," I say as I pick out a leather pouch and open it to reveal numerous orange capsules.

Theon and the other archangels look even worse than I remember, and we're quick to make the rounds, administering the medicine. I make sure to check every archangel to see if we're fated, but none of them are my mates.

Saphis visits the archangels in turn as well, only using his strength to heal the worst burn marks inflicted by the fish. He even heals most of Nate's burn marks as well.

It's not long before the archangels look like they're in much better health, and Theon suggests we stick together for a while, but there's no point in them following us. After taking two blades to replace the ones I'd lost, I instruct them to take the provisions and find somewhere to relax and recover while they wait for this ordeal to be over.

Prince Callan has a private word with the archangels, and I expect him to remain with them, but when Nate, Shade, and I start walking down the street, he follows.

"You can stay with them, you know," I say, when he catches up to us. "When I find my other mates, we'll come back for you." I don't bring up the fact that he doesn't want to bond with me. I'm still hoping that by then he will change his mind.

"If the archangels were that bad, I can only imagine what the other alphas in the city must be experiencing now. They're going to end up killing each other," Prince Callan says, instead of acknowledging what I've said.

"Or us," Nate comments, twirling a blade in his hand. One that he also snagged from the chest.

Prince Callan's expression is unreadable. "I think it's better if I stay with you until this ordeal is over."

I'm silent as I think about what he's really just said. That he's going to stick around to make sure I don't die a true death. Because if I do, he'll have to endure emptiness for the rest of his life. I sigh. There was a brief moment when we were in the water that I told myself he was there for me. Not just because he knows what will happen if I die, but that he was there for *me*. That was, until reality sunk in, and I knew he was just there to avoid my death and for the medicine. I can't even be upset at him for it. As a royal, I understand what it's like. Having that responsibility for your subjects. In any case, if it weren't for him, I might not have made it out. If it weren't for him, I could still be trapped down there.

"Thanks," I say softly. "For a moment there, I didn't think I was getting out."

Something flickers in Prince Callan's eyes. Anger, maybe? I can't tell.

"That monster," he replies, moving closer beside me. "I've heard tales about it. They say it can't be killed. That it's some kind of spirit from the shadow realm."

"Something like that," I mutter.

"Why would the king bring it here? Why would he make you face that?"

"Who knows why the king does anything?" I say wearily, though I've been wondering the same thing. I'd been so sure that there must have been a weapon in the chest that would have helped me defeat the monster, but there wasn't. So how had Dad expected me to best that thing?

Prince Callan doesn't look impressed by my answer. "I don't think I'll ever understand your family."

"Yeah, I wouldn't try if I were you. Sometimes you just have to accept your family for what it is."

He gives me a strange look then, though I'm not sure why. Probably because his family is awesome and nowhere near as messed up as my non-existent mother and overbearing father who loves psychotic games.

"And if I ask you why the king is retiring," Prince Callan says slowly, not taking his gaze from my face. "I gather you'll give me the same answer?"

My brow creases as the exhaustion from my time in the water weighs on me. My body has already healed completely, but emotionally, I'm still a mess. "He's over a thousand years old," I reply. "I'd like to hope that eventually I'll be able to retire as well."

It's not exactly a lie, but I get the feeling the prince knows I'm not truly answering his question. In any case, he doesn't continue to pry, and I turn my attention back to the city, my thoughts wandering to the strange glowing fish in the bathhouse. Their words echo in my head: *Still lost.*

FOURTEEN

~ Nate ~

When I'd first realized the princess is my mate, I knew it would complicate things. Even so, I'd been sure that once we returned to the palace and I had my hands on the treasure, it wouldn't matter. Even if we bonded, her other mates could take care of her when I left.

But when she'd been sucked beneath the water in the bathhouse, well, I'd never before experienced the stab of fear that had almost crippled me.

I'd stumbled to the edge of the bath, limping from the agony of my burns, and I'd stared into the watery depths contemplating jumping in. *Nine Lives.* That's what the angels in Toralyn called me, but I knew if I went into that water again, I wouldn't have emerged. I was already weakened, and the fish still glowed close to the surface of the water, like guard dogs who refused to let me pass.

Prince Callan paced as I went in and out of consciousness, and I knew he was as conflicted as I was, but when the fish finally moved away to the other side of the bath, he shouted something at me and dived in.

By now, my body had transformed back, and I stayed by the edge of the water, determined to stay conscious as I waited for what felt like an eternity. Too long. They were in the water for too fuckin' long, but then they were there, gasping as they broke the surface.

I didn't want to acknowledge the relief I felt, but it took everything in me not to cradle my queen to my body. I wanted to stroke my hands through her hair, to touch every part of her, and to tear apart whatever had harmed her, but instead, I simply watched intently.

Ah fuck, I'm in trouble, I think as I force my thoughts back to the present. The princess hardly says a word as we walk past buildings, meet alphas, and navigate the maze of streets. On the outside, she's as sassy and feisty as ever, but I didn't survive this long without learnin' how to read others. Something is bothering her, and the thought makes my inner beast unsettled.

I tear my gaze from her face now as we walk, and I point to a large house not far from us. The walls look solid despite the layer of black covering the bricks, and I can't detect any alphas nearby.

"Let's stop here for a while. I could use the rest," I say, pretendin' I'm only thinking of myself. Whatever happened in the water has affected her more than she'll admit, and I get the feelin' this female is even more stubborn than I am.

"For once, I agree with Nine Lives," Prince Callan drawls.

To my relief, the princess nods absently and heads in that direction. The two-story house looks much the same as the others on this street, with a wide entranceway and dead vines crawling up the side of the building. The place is empty, and I follow Blake into the living room at the front. "I'll take the first watch," I volunteer. Truthfully, after the archangel healed me, I feel better than I have in quite a while.

Blake opens her mouth to protest, but Shade squawks in agitation, and Blake sighs. "Fine, but we're only stopping for a few hours, and then we're continuing on."

She moves to the broken couch across the room and dusts off the aged material. Then, maneuvering her body, she begins peeling off her wet clothes and hanging them out to dry. The archangel turns, giving her privacy, but I stand there gaping like a dumb fuck who has yet to bed his first female. It's not until she turns, her fingers stilling on the straps of her pants, that I mumble about walking the perimeter.

By the time I return minutes later, the princess is

asleep, and the archangel is watching over her with a severe expression on his face.

"Careful prince, you're startin' to act like you like her," I comment in a low voice as I stalk into the room.

"If things were different, I probably would," he admits, and I'm surprised by the sincerity in his voice. "Not that you can talk. Don't think I haven't noticed the way you've been glancing at her. Are you serious about wanting to live in her palace?"

Guilt makes my stomach roil. "It'd be an easy life."

He sighs. "Life as a royal is many things, but it's not easy." Then as if he realizes he's just confessed that out loud, he clears his throat and turns to me. "You might want to work on that lie if you expect her to believe it. I don't know what you're hoping to get from her, but if you try to harm our mate, I'll happily put you back in your place."

"I don't doubt that, prince. I haven't forgotten what you did in Toralyn."

He looks at me strangely for a moment before turning his attention back to the princess.

"What about you?" I prompt. "What are your plans when it comes to the princess?"

I know his response before he even opens his mouth.

"You know why I can't," he replies coldly, his gaze as hard as stone. I would regret asking him if I didn't remember what an asshole he is.

"I'll be on the roof," I grumble, leaving the room.

~

~ Princess Blake ~

Neither Prince Callan nor Nate are there when I wake, but Shade is perched on the back of the couch, and she peers my way as I sit up.

Yawning, I stretch out my limbs. *"How long was I out?"*

"I'm guessing around three hours."

"Three hours?" I yawn again and my mouth is wide open when the familiar scent of chocolate reaches my nose. It's the same smell from when I exited the bathhouse, and I snap my mouth shut, scanning the room.

"Everything okay?" Shade asks, picking up on my unsettled energy.

I narrow my eyes, my gaze flitting over the broken furniture. *"Has anyone else been in here?"*

"You mean aside from your mates who are trying their hardest to pretend they don't want you, even when it's obvious they want to bury their faces into your vagina?"

"What?"

"What?" she parrots.

I groan. I can't deal with her rambling right now. *"Never mind. I'm probably just imagining things."*

My stomach growls, and I lift from the couch and dress. The satchel of provisions is close by, and I grab out a parcel of dried bread, and make my way from the room, deciding to explore the house while I eat. I tell myself it's not because I'm trying to avoid the others, but I don't know who I'm trying to fool.

Shade perches on my shoulder as we make our way through the rooms on the ground floor. There's not much to see. Charred walls. Broken pottery. The occasional scorched piece of furniture. We enter a room that has some kind of ancient burner in one corner, and I can only guess the space was designed as some kind of kitchen. The thought of a freshly cooked meal makes my stomach ache, despite the bread ration that I finished off while in the last room.

I sigh, knowing I should take over on watch duty so that one of the guys can get some rest. I'm about to leave the room when a piece of pottery buried in a pile of ash and dirt catches my eye. Bending, I pick up the rounded clay wedge and blow on it. The piece is charred, but the image of a winged bird is only just visible beneath the black.

When I go to put it back on the ground, I notice more shattered pottery closer to the wall. Likely, they're all pieces from the same vase or bowl, but it's not the clay shards that have my attention now. Amidst the pottery is a distinct black ring made of steel.

Squatting down, I brush away the dust and ash.

"Oh crap, is that what I think it is?" Shade practically squawks in my mind.

"I think so." I brush my hand over the metal and

hook two fingers into the ring and pull. The trap door comes free, dust pluming in the air as I reveal a set of stairs that leads down into darkness.

Shade swallows. *"We're not going down there, are we? Can't we just close it and pretend we don't know it's there?"*

"What? Aren't you curious? We can't simply turn around now."

"Uh, yes girl, we can. In fact, let me show you." She adjusts her feet and pivots her body so she's facing backwards on my shoulder and looking back toward the doorway.

I grin. *"If you want to go, you can. But I need to know what's down there."*

I can practically hear her groan in my head, but she doesn't fly off. *"If I die, I want the record to state that this* was *your bright idea."*

"Done."

Still grinning, I pull out one of my daggers and take a tentative step onto the first stair. It holds, the stone keeping intact beneath my feet, and I take two more steps. As I move, small yellow lights flare to life on the stairs like little glowing stars, lighting my way down. I'm on my tenth step, able to see dim shadows when light explodes around us, bright bulbs glowing brightly and buzzing where they're suspended from the ceiling. Shade jumps on my shoulder, and I lift a hand to steady her.

"What is this place?" I say aloud in awe as I stare at what appears to be some kind of bunker. The air is cool and musty, and the walls of the space are covered in the most beautiful paintings I've ever seen. My eyes take in a forest filled with flowers and birds of every color of the rainbow. On another wall there's a large fountain where water spurts from the mouths of stone fish, and on the floor near my feet is the depiction of two wings stretched out in front of a sun. It almost looks like some kind of family crest, similar to what each of the demon clans in Seral have.

Around the room, there are two chaise lounges, a marble table and chairs, and three doors leading to separate areas. I investigate what's behind each door to find a room with two beds still dressed with sheets, some kind of antique washroom, and what looks to be a storage room with shelves packed with decorated pots. Everything is covered in a thick coat of dust, but there's no ash, no blast damage. "It's some kind of survival room," I murmur out loud, hardly able to believe what I'm seeing. "I've always wondered, always *hoped* that maybe some of the beings in Perstalia survived."

"This is amazing," Shade says carefully, *"but even if there were beings down here once, they're not here now. If anyone had survived, we would know by now."*

The reality of her words dims my excitement. Because even if beings had survived down here, when they finally ventured to the surface again there would have been nothing for them. And without food and water they would have had no hope. But I still feel like finding this place, with the paintings preserved, feels like a win. Satisfaction goes through me at the idea that the witches didn't destroy everything. I'm not sure why it means so much to me. Maybe because with the witches infiltrating Seral City, I worry we could end up like Perstalia. But this… My excitement rises again when I think about the fact there could be more undiscovered bunkers around the city. Due to the toxicity of the city, as far as I know the city has hardly been explored, but now that we're aware of the bunkers, maybe I can set up a team of demons to do some exploration.

Shade flaps from my shoulder, resting on the silver chaise lounge. *"I'll say one thing. It's nice to see more useable furniture for a change."*

I smile as I turn and sheathe my dagger, focusing on the painting of the forest. The brush strokes of the leaves are flawless, the different shades of green blending together. *"Check this out, Shade. It's so lifelike."*

When she doesn't respond, I turn my head. *"Are you all right there, or is it too much—"* The words die in my throat when I glimpse her laying unnaturally still on the lounge, her eyes closed and toes curled. And then I smell it. The faint scent of chocolate touches the air, the bitter sweetness at odds with the damp, musty room. The alluring smell makes my body loosen, but I know better. A whistling sounds to my right, and I drop down in time to avoid the throwing star that was aimed at my neck. The blade clangs as it collides with the stone wall behind me and drops to the ground.

More whistling sounds, and I spring into action,

narrowly dodging three more stars that fly at me from seemingly nowhere.

"Show yourself," I snarl, landing in a crouch.

There's a pause, and I draw my dagger as an abnormally tall, cloaked figure materializes from behind the lounge. Despite his size, his movements are agile, and he sends three more stars my way in rapid succession. I maneuver out of the way, catching the last star in mid-air before it can soar past my head. Flicking my wrist, I send it back toward the figure, and it tears through the flap of his cloak. The blade doesn't hit flesh, but my attacker gives a grunt of surprise and satisfaction rolls through me. I scan the distinct tribal tattoos on his bare arms, the inked circles and runes forming a familiar pattern.

My eyes widen. "You're a Drozac. One of the legendary assassins from Rostof." I say it as more of an accusation than a question.

The figure doesn't respond, but I see it in his cool gray eyes. The swirling hatred and cold, calculated intelligence. The Drozac are ruthless and never miss their target once they've been assigned one. Unfortunately for this guy, I'm about to sully his reputation.

"You shouldn't have touched my friend," I growl. "What did you do to her?" Shade can't have been his target, but I don't think the Drozac worry themselves about collateral damage. I think about the other times I've detected the scent of bitter chocolate, and the chilling realization that this male has been following us makes my anger rise. *He targeted Shade because he sees her as my weakness.*

The cloaked figure pulls out a dagger and rushes at me, but I'm quick to react, blocking his strikes and sending out a few of my own. I note the way the assassin carefully keeps his distance. He's well-trained, able to deflect each of my moves, and his blade slices across my chest, cutting through my shirt and drawing blood.

I take a step back, but I don't bother looking at the damage. My skin is already knitting back together. "If she's dead, I won't just kill you," I say as I eye my attacker. "But you already know that, don't you, Drozac?" I wonder what he's seen while he's watched me, and my thoughts go to Nate and Prince Callan. *Fuck. Are they dead?* I remind myself that if they were, I would have felt it, but panic still rushes through me.

The Drozac assassin's gaze remains hard. I can only make out his stubbled chin, straight nose, and gray eyes, but it's enough that I recognize him—the cloaked giant I glimpsed in the ballroom.

"I only plan to take one life today, and it's not that of the bird," he speaks for the first time, his rough voice making my stomach twist. Relief nearly crushes me. Shade's not dead. Nate and Callan, they're all fine. *Thank Lady Fate, they're alive.* I only give myself seconds to let the news sink in, and then I'm back to glaring at the Drozac assassin. "You should have known better than to attack me like this," I say, wishing I could see more of his face. "Now the Drozac will lose yet another brother." I vaguely wonder why the assassin didn't kill me while I was sleeping, but he lunges for me, raw hatred burning in his eyes.

Before he reaches me, I kick out, knocking his blade from his hand, and spinning before sweeping his feet out from under him. He falls onto his back, and before he can flip back up, I'm on him, straddling him with my blade pressed to his throat. The skin of his neck bulges just above his Adam's apple, turning white at the pressure.

I lean in close, forcing all of my weight onto him, and almost stop breathing when his scent crashes into me. *Holy Fuck.* The distinct sweet bitterness of chocolate invades my senses, mixing with the scent of cool, crisp mint. My inner muscles clench, my body lighting on fire as everything in me tells me that he's mine. *No. It can't be.* I want to deny it, but he smells too good, and my stomach growls at the thought of tasting him and touching him. Desire rolls through my body making my every nerve come alive.

The hood of his cloak falls back, and my lips part in surprise as I finally stare at his face. The male is sexy as fuck with a chiseled jawline, deep-set gray eyes under dark brows, and defined cheekbones. His thick brown hair is tied behind his head, and he looks just as stunned as I feel.

"Get off me, Enchantress," he breathes, his voice low and gruff, and I hate the way it makes my stomach squeeze as I become all too aware of him between my legs. He tries to push up, but I plant my palm on his chest, pressing him back down as I keep my blade to his throat.

No, this can't be right. I know Lady Fate sometimes makes questionable match-making decisions but to choose a member of the Drozac as one of my mates is simply ridiculous. I lean closer to him, hoping that somehow, I'm wrong. I sniff him again, and another wave of desire makes me bite my lip. *Nope. Not wrong. Well, fuck.*

"What are you doing?" he growls, but I press my blade harder against his throat, silencing him.

"Hoping that my sanity will return any moment now," I retort. "Now shut up while I try to figure this out." I can't kill him. Not if he's my mate. But—

With more strength than I'm expecting, he throws me off him, and I fly back into the wall, right into the painting of the forest. The stone cracks at the impact, along with my back, and I sag as I breathe through the pain. My body tingles, already healing in the seconds that follow, but then he's there, his hot breath puffing on my face as he presses his tattooed forearm under my chin, squeezing my neck. I glimpse the silver cuffs around his wrists. I'd been so distracted with the fact that he's my mate, that I'd forgotten he might use his power on me. Only the Drozac can harness the strength of their giant form while still remaining in their smaller size.

I should be angry, but even now while he's choking me, his scent swirls in the air making my head light. The image of his hands wrapped around my neck while he pounds into me pops into my head, and I whimper. That's right. I fucking *whimper.*

Heat flushes his cheeks, and he leans into me, his knee pressing hard between my thighs. I struggle to keep back a moan, and his nostrils flare. Blood trails from the corner of my mouth, and I lick at it, smiling at him.

"Great temptress," he curses under his breath, his chest heaving.

His arm loosens under my neck, and I see my moment. I swing him around, slamming his back against the wall as I pin him there. My demon strength can't match that of his giant form, but he only glares at me as he remains in my hold. The heat in his eyes vanishes, and he glowers at me like I'm everything he hates. I think about the Drozac assassin who had been captured in Seral years ago. The king hadn't been merciful, and his death had been a warning to the other Drozac never to venture into our land.

But we aren't in Seral anymore.

The assassin growls as he pushes me off, tossing me onto the table which cracks at the impact, the legs giving way. And then he's above me, his thick thighs closing me in. His eyes flash with anger, and his face scrunches as if he's in pain as he pins me there. I'm sure he must know I'm his mate, but maybe that doesn't matter to a member of the Drozac?

"You can't kill me," I tell him, just in case he's not smart enough to have figured it out by now. "Just like I can't kill you."

His face reddens like he's struggling to control himself, and I actually feel sorry for him. His grip on my wrists loosens, and the look of pain in his expression intensifies. Seconds pass, and I'm almost certain he's about to bust a blood vessel in his left eye, but he suddenly moves off me, staggering back to the bottom of the stairs.

"Look, I get that you hate demons," I say slowly, "but we're going to have to figure this out. You must know I'm your mate."

His scowl only deepens, his jaw clenching. "Watch your back, Enchantress," he warns, and then he legs it up the stairs.

I sigh. *Great. This mate is another dud.*

FIFTEEN

~ Princess Blake ~

*E*nchantress? I'm not sure what the assassin is on about, but I don't try to stop him when he retreats. Mostly, because I'm not sure what to do about him yet. Instead, I rush to Shade's side, sitting on the lounge and cupping her in my hands. She feels so fragile, her feathers ruffled and body limp, but it's not long before she stirs.

"Blake?" she asks groggily, her black eyes blinking up at me.

I curse Lady Fate for making the Drozac assassin my mate. I should have killed him.

"You're okay," I say soothingly. *"It looks like he hit you with a sleeping drug."*

"He?"

"Sorry, while you were napping, I met another one of my mates. He's a member of the Drozac," I cringe as I explain.

"An assassin!" she gasps, struggling to get up, and I stroke her feathers until she calms.

"He won't kill me now that he knows we're fated," I assure her. *"Not that he could, even if he tried."* I think about his scent of bitter chocolate and crisp mint, and the memory of him between my legs makes me antsy.

"That also means you can't kill him," Shade points out.

There's a commotion upstairs, and Nate and Prince Callan appear, weapons in their hands. It's actually comical to see them rush down here so fast. Air swirls around the room, teasing my hair as Prince Callan stares at me and then at Shade. Moving past him, Nate prowls around the room, his eyes glinting like he's searching for his prey.

"You can relax," I tell them. "He's gone. At least, for now."

"Who is?" Prince Callan asks.

I sigh heavily. "Another one of my charming mates. Seems I'm mated to a Drozac assassin."

Nate frowns. "A Drozac? I thought those bastards can't have mates?"

"I don't know what to tell you, other than that Lady Fate must hate me," I reply. "I'm guessing I'm his target, but he's going to have to rethink those plans now that he knows I'm his mate."

Nate's lips twist into a smile. "There's never a dull

moment with you, is there, gorgeous?" His cat eyes flick to Shade. "She all right?"

Shade flutters her feathers, and I nod slowly. "Luckily for him."

"I never knew it would be so hard to keep a single female out of trouble," Prince Callan mutters, finally sheathing his sword and strolling around the room as the air settles. He studies the painting on the wall closest to him, his brow furrowing.

"I didn't know any of these bunkers existed," I say as I watch him walk beside the wall, taking it all in. "I thought everything was destroyed in the blast."

"Neither did I," Prince Callan replies. He disappears for a moment as he enters the bedroom, then he reappears again. "Everything here is well preserved."

"If this one exists, it's possible there could be more around the city," I say. "When this is all over, I'd like to get a team together to search for them and catalog what we find,"

Nate's eyes sparkle. "You think you might find something of worth?"

I arch my brow at the thief. "I think I might find out more about the beings who lived here. Aren't you curious about what they were like and how they lived? We don't even know what they looked like."

"I tend not to worry 'bout the dead, love," Nate replies as he flops onto the lounge beside me and drapes his arm behind my shoulders. "But I'll admit it's nice to be able to stay somewhere a little more accomodatin' for a change. So, now that you've found all your mates, who votes we stay here until King Dalton comes to collect us? It would beat movin' around the city."

I bite my bottom lip. *Three mates.* It's the most common number of fated mates for a powerful female, but for some reason, I don't feel like I've found everyone. And even if I have, I don't know where the Drozac assassin has disappeared to. I need him to complete the bonding ritual.

Nate goes on to say, "Your new friend will be back if that's what you're worried about. He won't be able to stay away." He must read the expression on my face then, because his brows rise and he goes onto add, "Unless you think you're tied to more?"

I brush my hair away from my face. "I have a feeling Lady Fate thinks I've got a thing for assholes, and she's not done with me yet."

Nate grins. "Then the hunt continues."

Prince Callan doesn't look impressed. Striding up the stairs I hear the trap door close, and a steel bar move into place. The archangel appears again a moment later, his face passive. "I need to rest before we move on. The door is reinforced and locked from the inside. This way we can get some shut eye without having to worry about any alphas or your new... friend." Then he makes his way toward the bedroom without another word and closes the door.

"One of these days I'm going to find out what his deal is," I send to Shade. When there's no reply, I peer down

to see she's fallen asleep in my hands. Reaching across, I place her on the lounge on my left side, keeping her tucked against the back of the chair. She's barely out of my hands when Nate closes in on my other side.

His warm, earthy scent washes over me, and I swallow hard. A low rumble starts in his chest as his reddish-gold eyes narrow, his gaze fixing on my lips.

"If you're getting ideas—" I start.

He gives me a predatory grin. "Course I am, my queen. You're my mate."

I try not to squirm with him this close to me. *Was it always this hot in here?* "You don't need to call me that, you know. I'm not even a queen yet."

"For my kind, we call our mates our queens," he explains.

Ah. Now that I didn't know. "And how can you be so sure we're mates?" I say. "Something tells me you're not the type of male to settle down."

His eyes flash. "And is that what you want? To settle down?"

I make a face. "What I want is to bond with my mates, so I have the power to keep the clan leaders in check. What I want is to make sure Seral doesn't turn into madness when Dad...uh...retires. Aside from that, nothing else matters."

"Then that's all you need to think about, gorgeous," he agrees, and he leans close, his lips colliding with my neck, and his hand sliding from the back of the lounge and winding around me, pulling me closer. Instinctively, I tip my head to the side, giving him better access, and he works up to my ear, his hot breath making me shiver.

"You want something, Nine Lives," I rasp, curving my back as my nerves come alive at his touch. "Something that's not me. And I'm going to find out what it is." I think about what Prince Callan has told me about him, and his reputation in Toralyn. He's not just a shifter, but a thief as well.

"Right now, all I want is you, demon," he says, biting my earlobe, and I moan at the scrape of his teeth.

Flipping my leg over, I straddle him, pressing onto his lap as his large hands slide across my back. The rumbling in his chest turns to a growl, and then my lips are on his, demanding that he respond. His scent wraps around me, driving me wild as I start to lose control, and his tongue dives into my mouth. I almost pull back at the unusual rough texture as his tongue tangles with mine, but he holds me firmly, his strong fingers pressing deliciously against me.

Breaking the kiss, I rock against him, enjoying the hard press of him between my thighs. He groans, his slitted eyes hooded as his hands move to my hips, forcing me to rub harder against him.

"So fuckin' sexy," he mutters as he sits up more, his lips moving to my collarbone as he drinks me in. My nipples harden, my body tightening even more at his words. I want this. *Fuck,* do I want this, but as one of his hands moves to the front of my pants Kai's face flashes in my mind, his stone-cold eyes wide and sightless. I jerk in Nate's hold, my chest heaving. I know I'm going to have to give in soon and test what happens when I'm with my mates, but my heart races at the thought of harming Nate.

"Wait," I gasp as the beast shifter's thumb hooks into the front of my pants. "We can't."

Nate's voice is a low rumble, thick with desire. "I've heard the rumors, gorgeous. Whatever happened, your last lover wasn't your mate."

He's right, but it's too late. I scramble off him, my legs feeling strange as I move away from his lap and take a step backward. "I just, can't yet."

His wide chest rises and falls as he watches me, his gaze predatory and carnal. The tips of fangs protrude from his mouth, and my core tightens when he licks his lips. His muscles coil like he's going to pounce for me, and my muscles twitch, but he doesn't move.

"I thought you want to seal the bond," he points out. "Think of this as practice."

I take another step back, though my legs feel heavy. "Just. Not now," I say, fully preparing myself to have to fight him off if needed.

He only grins, showing off his partially shifted teeth. "Whatever you wish, my queen," he purrs, and he lifts from the lounge and prowls over to the other couch, dropping down and closing his eyes like he intends to sleep.

I try to control my breathing as I fight against the urge to follow him and pick up where we left off. *Fuck.* I can't deny that he's mine, but the thought of accidentally killing my jaguar mate makes my stomach want to reject the last thing I ate.

Not yet, I tell myself. When I find all my mates, then we can test the theory of what happens when we're together.

I sit there for a long while thinking about the assassin and my other mates and how we're possibly going to figure this all out, but eventually I lift from the lounge and venture into the storage room. Rows of colored clay pots line the shelves against the walls of the small room, and I take my time peering into each pot. They're all empty except for dried remnants on the bottom of some of them, and it makes me wonder how long the owners of the bunker were down here for. Did they stay here for as long as possible before they were forced to surface? Peering around, I don't detect any kind of ventilation system that would have allowed them to breathe for a long period of time, but I don't spend long searching. For all I know, the beings that lived here didn't need to breathe.

A thud from somewhere in the bunker has me drawing my dagger and rushing back to the living room. I scan the area, half expecting the assassin to be there even though I know the door is locked, but the space is quiet. Shade sleeps peacefully on the lounge, and Nate's chest rises and falls steadily as he relaxes unaware of whatever had made the noise. The washroom is also empty, and I creep into the bedroom where Prince Callan retreated. There's still no sign of the Drozac assassin or anything that could have made the noise, but the prince is resting on one of the beds. His eyes remain closed as I move over to him, staring at the sleeping archangel.

He's breathtaking to look at, the shimmering gold of his wings making him seem more like a sculpture than a living male. Compelled by the invisible bond between us, I lean closer, dragging in his scent of green apples and bergamot. His smell is addictive, and I fight against the urge to move nearer to him, my gaze fixing on his gold-brushed lips.

Keep it together, Blake, I mentally hiss at myself, but I can't stop myself from reaching out, sliding a finger along the ribbed membrane of his golden wings. He shivers, his muscles tightening, but before I can move away his hand flies up, clamping around my wrist.

Hazel eyes rimmed with gold stare up at me, and my heart lurches as he stares, lust clouding his gaze. His attention shifts, his gaze dropping from my face to where he's still holding my hand suspended in the air.

I come to my senses faster than he does, and I yank my hand free and take a large step back, feeling like I can breathe again.

He watches me carefully, his expression hardening though the lust never leaves his eyes.

"Is there...something I can help you with?" he drawls, his throat bobbing as he speaks.

"You could start by telling me why you're such an ass," I blurt, frustration winding through me.

He blinks like he's surprised by my comment, but then his mask slips into place, that cool, casual demeanor taking over his features. "You're a royal, you know how these things work. We don't get the luxury of indulging in our..." he pauses, his gaze heating again as he stares at me, "fantasies."

My cheeks warm. *Fantasies?* "I'm your fated mate," I say incredulously. "No one goes against the mate bond. Don't you want to unlock your power?"

He holds my gaze, and I swear I see a flicker of longing in his eyes. "Since when has this life ever been about what I want?"

My heart pounds. "And what is it that you want?"

His lips part, and for a brief moment, I think he's going to tell me. That he's going to let me in, but then his lips curve into a forced smile. "To be reunited with my subjects in Toralyn. I imagine it must be the same for you. Surely, you're keen to be back with the demons."

I stare at him. *Toralyn.* All he can think about is going back there. Back to whatever or whomever has already captured his heart. I haven't heard of anyone loving someone else more than their fated mate, but I guess there's a first for everything.

"Right," I say hastily. "Of course." I'm not lying, because I do want to get back to Seral. I'd been forcing myself not to think about the witches infiltrating the city and the king's fatal disease, but every night we're away I wonder whether things are worsening in the demon realm. I don't point out to Prince Callan that the king isn't going to be happy when he hears the archangel prince doesn't want to complete the mate bond. That's a problem for another time. I turn toward the door, but Prince Callan's next question stops me.

"You controlled those fish, didn't you?" he says as he sits up, leaning on his elbows. "When we were in the bath."

I turn back to peer at him. "I like to think of it more as, I asked nicely and they listened." I figure there's no point lying, even if the guy does want to pretend we're not fated mates.

His expression is thoughtful, but he doesn't question me further, so I slip from the room.

SIXTEEN

~ Alaric ~

I make my way to an abandoned building down the street and slide into the darkness between the stone walls. *Enchantress.* That's what I'd called the demon princess when she'd been close to me, her small form trapped beneath my body. I think about my knee pressed against her and the way her lips had parted, need flushing her face. Gods her scent had all but driven me mad as the desire to take her made me start to unravel.

I clench my hands into fists, leaning against the cool stone of the building and letting it ground me. I can't lose control. Not now when I'm finally close to getting revenge for my brother. I've killed females before. As a member of the Drozac, when I'm given a kill order I don't ask questions. I find my target and I end them efficiently and quietly, but this female... The moment we'd locked eyes in the ballroom, I'd known she was different. Sticking to the shadows, I've been observing her ever since she left the ancient theater. Even without speaking to her, it was clear she's a temptress. Just the sight of her always made my blood pound harder. I shouldn't have been surprised. I expected no less from the daughter of the feared demon king himself.

Look we're going to have to figure this out. You must know I'm your mate. Her poisonous words repeat in my mind, but I purge the lie. I won't let her get the better of me. Whatever my reaction to the female, we can't be mates. It's well-known that those sworn to the order of the Drozac don't get mates. We give up that right when we chant our oaths and send our vows to Lady Fate herself. And now it's been over a decade that I've waited for this moment. For this chance to make things right. Blood for blood.

I think about the shifter thief and archangel prince who have been staying close to the princess. They believe they're her mates going by what I've picked up from their conversations, but it's hard to know whether she's simply enchanted them as well. Either way, an uncomfortable feeling swirls in my gut at the idea of the three of them together, and I clench my fists tighter. *No, those males aren't her mates, and neither am I. She's just keeping us under her spell. Maybe she isn't even half angel but half witch.* My scowl deepens at the thought. The only beings I hate more than the demons are the witches...and the leaders of the order of the Drozac.

My chest squeezes as I picture my twin brother, West's, face. Only the elite are chosen to be members of the Drozac, the guild of assassins in Rostof, and I remember the day West was selected. The tattooed figures who'd appeared on our doorstep with the message of his selection looked like they'd walked straight from the shadow realm, but West had been ecstatic. He'd believed their propaganda and the idea that it was an honor to be among the chosen. I'd begged him not to complete the ritual. Not to sign up for the order, but he did it anyway. In the years that followed, when he'd finally seen the true heart of the order and realized his mistake, it was too late.

Despite swearing his allegiance and agreeing to disown all ties to family and friends, he defied the order in secret, meeting up with me once every year after the harvest. For one night, he'd allow himself to laugh with me like we were young again.

Until he never turned up. It took me a year to break into the highly defended assassin guild tower and find the information that detailed his demise. He'd been on a mission in Seral to kill one of the higher clan leaders. It had been a case of bad luck that King Dalton had made an unexpected appearance at the clan house right as West was about to make the killing blow. The clan leader was saved, and my brother was murdered instead.

That night in the tower, my eyes had devoured the words on the papers, rage boiling within me as I read on, and I'd stayed longer than I knew I should. At that point I didn't care. When they found me, I took down four assassins until one of the masters brought me to my knees.

I thought my life would end then. I *wanted* it to end, but instead of executing me, they assessed the carnage in my wake and offered me something I couldn't refuse instead. *Revenge.* All I had to do was take the oath to become a member of the Drozac and one day I would get my revenge on King Dalton and the demons. So for decades I trained and carried out orders without question. Because only one thing mattered, and it wasn't the lives of the cruel nobles that I took.

When word of the demon king's invitation spread throughout Rostof, I was the one who approached the masters with a proposal for a kill order. It wasn't how the process was usually carried out, but I'd long-since known there were issues between the giants and demons, with the last round of negotiations going poorly. If I take out the demon princess, Seral will be thrown into chaos, and then I'll take out King Dalton when he's stricken with grief.

Except I hadn't counted on the fact that the demon princess isn't just a demon. She's more than that, and whatever powers she wields, it's starting to make me question everything I thought I knew. Even as an intense hatred makes my body sweat, I can still smell her on my skin, and her scent is like a weapon disarming me. *Fuck.* I shake my head as if to clear it and push off from the wall. It doesn't matter how my body responds to her enchantments, her life is mine.

SEVENTEEN

~ Princess Blake ~

Nate yawns as we step into the ruined kitchen, and he adjusts the strap of the leather satchel on his shoulder. "You sure we have to leave now?" Twisting his head, he peers longingly at the stairs leading back to the furnished bunker. "Cats like their sleep, you know."

"Well, you're welcome to remain here," Prince Callan suggests, looking a little too eager for Nate to take him up on the offer.

The jaguar shifter turns his attention to the prince. "And leave my queen alone with you? I might be a thief, but I'm not an idiot."

"Now that is debatable," Prince Callan mutters.

Shade tilts her head as she watches them. *"I swear*

they've both been extra irritable since they woke," she comments. *"You let them rest for hours, and yet, it's like they're children who are grumpy after waking from a nap."*

I blow out a breath, but I don't tell her about my recent encounters with Nate and Prince Callan. Instead, I'm distracted by the large black feather I spot amidst the shards of broken pottery not far away. *That's two feathers I've lost.* I try to tell myself it's normal for angels, but it's starting to feel like a bad omen. *Great. Just one more thing I have to deal with.* I make a point not to draw attention to it, because the last thing I need is for Shade to worry, and I start walking while Nate and Prince Callan are still arguing. They follow after me, and I'm glad when no one mentions the feather.

It's night when we emerge from the house, and I hum as I enjoy the feel of the cool crisp air kissing my skin. It's not quite the same as a night in Seral city, the surrounding buildings silent and abandoned, but it's nice to have fresh air again.

We walk for what feels like an hour, and I'm starting to get worried at the fact we haven't encountered any alphas when I hear the faint sound of singing on the wind. "Do you hear that?" I whisper, changing direction and heading toward the voices.

"Yes, it sounds like a wailing cat." Prince Callan nods, his hand already resting on the hilt of his sword.

Nate's brows pull down. "I'll have you know a cat's wail sounds nothing like that strange garbling. In fact, I'll demonstrate." He sucks in a deep breath, but I wack him on the chest, and he doubles over as the air rushes from between his lips.

I give him a sheepish smile, realizing I hit him harder than I intended. "Sorry, but the last thing we need is to announce our location to everyone in this city."

"Fair point," he mutters as he straightens.

Prince Callan smirks and links his arm with mine, leading me toward the noise.

I slow our pace. "Hold on, I think we should go over some ground rules before we go any further. By now the alphas who haven't gotten their hands on any medicine are going to be hallucinating and out of their minds." I remember the heads Nate and Prince Callan brought to me as presents not too long ago. "Even if they don't turn out to be my mates, you can't just kill them all."

Prince Callan frowns.

"Got it. Incapacitate but don't kill," Nate says, his eyes bright like simply the idea of a fight has improved his mood significantly.

I figure that's a good enough response and continue walking toward the singing that's grown even louder. Truthfully, Prince Callan's assessment wasn't too far off. It sounds like something between the cry of a wounded animal and the mating call of a group of demon bugs, and the closer we get, the more I start to question my life choices. Knowing my luck, I'm probably fated to whatever delightful minstrel is leading this musical disaster.

We reach a wide stretch of dirt with multiple stone paths branching off, and blackened trees that look like skeletons spread throughout the area. I can only guess it used to be a city park at one stage, going by the layout and various stone fountains erected at intervals, and I start walking again.

Shade is silent on my shoulder as she watches the trees, and I wonder if she's thinking about the lack of birds. The park is a far cry from the beautiful nature scenes we've seen depicted in the paintings around the city.

"Well, they sound happy," Nate comments, and I jerk my attention forward as we round a bend, passing a thick section of blackened trees. Up ahead, beside the largest stone fountain we've seen yet, I make out a group of twenty demons dancing around a roaring fire. Shadows flicker around them like creatures from the shadow realm, and their singing has been replaced by raucous laughter. They're all shirtless, their muscles rippling in the firelight, and their tails flick as if in time to music only they can hear. Two of them I recognize as clan leaders, but the others are the sons of wealthy merchants and business owners. I grin, glad that they're not killing each other. "At least someone's enjoying this."

"Yes, they seem like they're in unusually good spirits for alphas who have been stranded in Perstalia," Prince Callan observes. He reaches for his sword, but I pin him with a stare.

"It's not a crime to be happy," I tell him. "Remember, no bloodshed unless necessary."

He smirks like I've just given him a challenge he can't resist, but he removes his hand from the hilt of his sword. "Something tells me it's going to be necessary."

I give him an unimpressed look. *"This is going to go terribly, isn't it?"* I say to Shade.

"Yum." There's a pause. *"Oh, I mean, yup. Yup it is."* Her gaze is fixed on the demons up ahead, and I shake my head.

"Please don't drool on my shoulder," I tease.

"Luckily for you, birds don't drool," she quips back. She's barely finished saying it when one of the demons completely undresses himself and starts dancing stark naked. She startles on my shoulder letting out a squawk of surprise, and I burst out laughing. She pecks my neck in retaliation.

"Stop!" I laugh, tucking my chin to stop her from tickling me.

"Uh, gorgeous, you might want to..." Nate trails off, and my laughter instantly dies as I straighten. The demons have stopped dancing, and they're all facing our direction, staring straight at me. *Crap.* Clearing my throat, I lift my chin as my strides eat up the last of the distance between us.

The demons form up respectfully when I stop a few steps away from them, and Nate and Prince Callan flank me.

"Our princess," the demon closest to me slurs with a dip of his horned head. "It is good to see you well."

I note how calm they are. A couple are unsteady on their feet, and a few are splattered with blood, but they don't look like demons who have lost their minds.

"Blake, look," Shade whispers, right as I spot the heads. Near the back of the fountain and shrouded in darkness are three giant hydra heads sitting in a pool of green ichor. Their fanged mouths are gaping open, their eyes wide and sightless. I'd been so distracted by the laughing demons that I hadn't even noticed. The rest of the hydra's body is nowhere to be seen, and I scan the area, my hand reaching for my sword.

"It's dead," says a familiar smooth voice that I know all too well. "The stones of the fountain shifted, taking the slain monster below. Same thing happened with the other monster at the fountain further to the west across the park."

I lift my gaze as my own personal pain-in-the-ass steps into view. A devilish smile is molded to his face and his eyes shine iridescent blue in the firelight, his horns mimicking the color and contrasting against his midnight hair. Despite myself, my chest eases at the sight of his familiar face. "Dante," I say the word on an exhale.

"The one and only," he grins, his eyes traveling over me. "Nice to see you finally found us, your highness."

"Found you? Funny, here I was thinking you might be trying to find me."

"Seeing as you're the one who can fly, we figured this was the smartest option." His gaze flicks to my mates with interest, and then back to me. "Though, now I'm starting to wonder whether I made a mistake. I'm not keen on the idea that you've been having fun without me."

I roll my eyes. "The only ones having fun on this little adventure seems to be you demons. I'm glad you found yourself some provisions." Scattered around the fire are a few wine bottles and other supplies, and now that I'm paying more attention, I can scent the alcohol on the demons even from here.

"The creatures put up a fight," another alpha explains, "but they weren't a match for us." He lifts his fist into the air as he says the last part, and the others all cheer, their faces flushed as they shout obscenities at the hydra and at whatever other monster they'd slain across the park.

Dante doesn't join them in celebration and watches me carefully. "So, I see you've already found two mates," he comments when their cheering dies down again.

"Three actually," I point out, "but it looks like Lady Fate isn't done with me yet."

His lips curve upward. "Then there's still hope for us."

The demons around him start grinning wider and leer at me.

"So, there is. I must say, I'm impressed you haven't all killed each other yet." Mostly, I'm surprised certain demons didn't use this as an opportunity to upset the power balance in Seral.

From the glint in Dante's eyes, I can tell he gets what I'm hinting at. "We all agreed we have a common goal," he explains. "There's plenty of time for us to be at each other's throats when we're back in Seral. Besides, we realized you might be upset if any of us accidentally killed one of your mates."

Smart. I have to give Dante credit for keeping the alphas in line. *I swear the demon has a silver tongue.* I smile. "Upset, is putting it mildly."

Dante nods, and there's a twinkle in his eye as he assesses Nate and Prince Callan. I can't shake the feeling he's judging me for all the times I broke up his orgies. Guess I can't talk now that I'm creating my own damn harem.

"Well, if you're done talking, I think it's time I find out if any of you guys have made the cut," I say.

Dante waves his hands graciously to the other alphas around him, and I ignore his arrogant smirk as I walk up to the first demon. Charzel, his name is. The stocky demon is the leader to one of the clans in the south-west of Seral City, and he has a reputation for being untrustworthy, probably because he's a powerful shapeshifter. As I step close to him there's the barest hint of fear in his charcoal eyes, like he thinks I might kill him if he doesn't turn out to be my mate. Shade's hard stare likely isn't helping his situation, and he refuses to look at her like he thinks she's about to crow and sentence him to death.

"Ooh, I love it when they can't meet my eyes," Shade says like she's on some kind of power high.

"Really, because I remember not too long ago when you enjoyed the attention from Nate."

"That's because he's delicious," she defends. *"This guy looks like he's about to soil his pants."*

My top lip curls at the thought, and the alpha's smile falls. He tenses like he thinks I'm about to strike, but I smooth my features. His weak floral scent isn't terrible, but it does nothing for me. I take pity on him and move on to the next demon.

One by one I make the rounds, moving close and talking to the alphas, but none of them are my mates. I'm not too surprised. Many of them I've met in close quarters in the past, and it's likely that we'd have discovered our fated connection before now. Still, I thought I'd be mated to at least one demon. *Guess there are more demons still in the city.*

Sighing, I stop a few feet from Dante and cross my arms in front of my chest.

"Is it my turn already?" he says with a wicked smile.

"Not even Lady Fate herself would try to match you with someone," I comment, thinking about the many females he's already been with, including humans. "You did your duty by attending this thing, but you've fulfilled the expectations put on you."

Confusion crosses his face, and his smile wavers. "You think I'm here because of an obligation to attend?"

"Aren't we all?" I point out as I recall the way Dad told me about the ball. It's not like we volunteered for this. I mean, the alphas did, but not in the way that one volunteers for an activity like a pie eating competition. Without another word, I turn to go.

"Aren't you going to see if he's your mate?" Shade asks. *"Lady Fate has proven that she's a little crazy with her matches. I mean, you're mated to one of the Drozac for goodness sake!"*

"Princess," Dante calls after me, and it's the first time I've heard uncertainty in his usually confident voice.

I tilt my head to look back at him.

"My obligation isn't fulfilled until you know for certain that I'm not your mate. I'd hate for you to keep searching only to discover I was right in front of you."

When I don't continue to move away, his lips quirk upward like he thinks he's won, though truthfully, I never intended to leave without testing him. I just enjoy making him squirm.

"Fine," I say exaggeratedly and stride toward him. As I walk, he watches me with appreciation, taking note of the sway of my hips, and I'm not nearly as offended as I know I should be.

I'm a couple steps away, and I'm about to stop because I want to continue messing with him, but he steps forward closing the distance between us. He doesn't stop to scent me. His hand slides behind my back as he pulls me to him, and then his lips are on mine like he's decided that even if we're not mates, he's going to make me remember this moment.

My head tells me I should pull away. This is *Dante,* and he's made it clear that no single female will ever have his heart, but...my blood heats, my pulse quickening as his taste of cardamon and freshly grown apricots fills my mouth. *Apricots.* Like the ones that grow at the back of his clan house. Apricots. Like the ones I would sometimes steal from his trees, smuggling them to the palace where I'd practically moan as I devoured them. I think about all the times I'd visited that clan house over the past months. Years, even. Had it ever been the apricots, or was it always him? Shade flies from my shoulder as his scent engulfs me, and my body comes alive at his touch.

He pulls me tighter against him, breaking the kiss and moving his lips to my jaw. "I knew you were mine," he says in a low voice, his breath hot on my skin.

At his words, images of his orgies with the humans flash in my mind, and my eyes fly open, my hand reaching for a blade.

"Fuck." He staggers back in surprise and keeps eye contact with me as he removes the dagger I've just wedged into his side.

"That's for bedding all those humans when you knew we were fated," I tell him.

He gives me a seductive smile. "I didn't sleep with any humans. I merely lured you closer because I knew you hadn't figured it out yet."

My mouth opens and then closes again as I recall every time I'd visited his clan house over the past months. Each time I'd found demons from his house romping with a human, but...he'd always been watching. I'd assumed he'd either had his turn earlier, or he was hardcore into voyeurism and was planning to get involved after.

"*Wait, he brought the humans to Seral, knowing I'd visit him?*" I send to Shade, still not believing any of this.

"*Is it any less believable than being matched to a member of the Drozac?*" she responds dryly.

She has a point, but I only scowl at him, knowing that he's been messing with me these past months. "Aren't I the lucky she-demon," I say sarcastically.

He tosses me my dripping blade, and I catch it with one hand. Honestly, at this point I'm beyond annoyed at Lady Fate. First, she matched me with an archangel who doesn't want me, then a shifter thief, who I have a feeling wants too much from me, followed by an assassin who hates me, and now the demon who has a reputation that's dirtier than his wicked mouth, even if he didn't bed the humans.

"*What did I do wrong?*" I send to Shade. "*Because I'm clearly being punished.*"

She only laughs as if finding out I'm fated to Dante is great news.

"*Don't sound so happy,*" I scold. "*We both know he has baggage. He has probably broken the hearts of half the females in Seral city, and possibly even some of the males. The last thing I need is petty exes coming after me."*

"You're going to be the queen, Blake. No she-demon in her right mind is going to come after you. Not if they value their life anyway."

It's a fair point, but I'm still irritated.

"So, I guess there are four of us now," Dante says as he saunters past the other demon alphas and stands near Nate and Prince Callan like he belongs there. "Though, I still don't see the fourth."

"Don't worry, he's a great addition to our odd... group," Prince Callan says dryly.

Nate claps Dante on the back. "You'll love him."

Dante raises a brow at the shifter, and Nate grins.

I'm torn between feeling like I want to bone the lot of them or strangle them. *Such is my life.*

"I'm sure I will," Dante replies to Nate, then his gaze settles back on me. "Shall we drink to celebrate our new...friendship?"

I hesitate. I'm pretty keen to keep moving, but the other demons are all staring at me, waiting to hear my response, and the fire does look inviting.

I turn to Nate and Prince Callan, and when neither of them protest, I nod once. "Fine, but we're not staying for long."

CHAPTER

EIGHTEEN

~ Princess Blake ~

Dante hunts us down a bottle of wine that hasn't yet been drained, and we settle by the roaring fire. I sigh, enjoying the warmth and getting comfortable.

The other demons keep a respectful distance, but they soon go back to enjoying themselves. Two males sit beside the fountain and arm wrestle, shouting obscenities as they battle one another, and a few others cheer them on, jeering and laughing. I smile as I watch them.

"You could show them how it's done," Dante comments with a grin, and he gestures with his head to the demon on the right, whose biceps are twice as large as his opponent's. "No one is able to best Roken, and I fear it's getting to his head."

Dante drops down beside me, and his scent of apricots makes my head spin. I clear my throat. "I don't think it'd be nearly as fun for them if I joined," I reply with a smirk.

"Yeah, but it'd be fun for us to watch," Nate says eagerly.

I shake my head and turn back to the fire, stretching out my hands and warming my fingers. Dante holds out the wine bottle, and I grab it from him, taking a drink.

"So, now that you're here, is anyone going to tell me why you haven't fucked yet? I get you wouldn't have been able to bond, but your restraint is... confusing," Dante comments. His dark gaze is locked on me as he says it, and I splutter, choking on the wine.

"Maybe, I haven't been in the mood," I wheeze out when I can breathe again.

His devilish lips twitch. "Is that so?"

I force myself to stare at the fire and not the ridges of his muscled chest exposed by his unbuttoned shirt. "Mhmm," I mumble, and drink more wine. Because damn, if there was ever an occasion to drink, it's now.

Nate chuckles and stretches his arms. "What makes you so sure we haven't, demon?"

"Well, for one, she's sucking on that wine bottle like she's imagining it's someone's cock," Dante replies, and this time I spit wine into the fire making the flames crackle.

"I was not," I defend, glaring at him, and he smirks as he stares back at me.

Nate gestures his head to where Prince Callan is spinning the small knife he'd removed from his boot. "Well, would you want to fuck this one? Look at that wingspan. The male is compensatin' for something."

Prince Callan stops spinning his blade. "Says the male who's undoubtedly planning to use the princess for some hidden purpose of his."

And...that's my cue to leave. So much for thinking we could have a relaxing drink by the fire.

"I need to get some air," I tell Shade. *"Make sure Nate doesn't do anything stupid like try to arm wrestle Roken."* At that moment, the large demon shouts out in victory, having bested his opponent.

Shade settles on the ground, staring at Nate and Prince Callan with beady eyes. *"You can count on me,"* she replies.

I lift to my feet, my temperature rising as three pairs of eyes fix on me. "I'm going to keep watch," I mumble, turning from them and not waiting for a response before striding away from the fire and further into the park. When I reach a group of skeletal trees, I stop and close my eyes, breathing in the night air which is bliss against my cheeks. *Stupid fated mates. If I ever meet Lady Fate I'm going to ask her to rethink the whole fated mates thing. I was doing just fine before this whole ordeal, and I bet I could find a way to keep the clan leaders of Seral in check, even without my full power.*

Behind me, someone else moves from the group, but I don't look to see who it is. Seeing as Shade hasn't said anything, I assume it's not Nate going to cause a brawl. Demons hate losing, and something tells me Rokan wouldn't play fair.

Folding my arms in front of my chest, I open my eyes and focus on the long stretch of dirt and trees around me. I wonder if the Drozac assassin is out there watching. If he was with us, we could try to bond. Even now that I know Dante is my mate, I can't tell if he's the last one. Bonding is the only sure way to check whether I've found all my mates, but I doubt Prince Callan has changed his mind about bonding with me.

Movement some distance away near a tree has me squinting to try and see clearer, but I'm distracted when I sense motion behind me. Instinctively, I stiffen, my hand flying to the hilt of the dagger at my side. Before I can grab out the blade, the hard ridges of a warm body presses against my back, and long fingers curl over my hand.

"As much as I'm a fan of knife play, princess, you won't be needing that now," Dante chuckles in my ear, his scent of apricots and cardamon reaching my nose. *Damn apricots.* My mouth waters, my breath hitching at his close proximity. Twisting my head to the side, I peer at the empty space behind me. It's a strange sensation, feeling someone even when you can't see them. I look further back to where Prince Callan, Nate, and Shade are still by the fire along with the rest of the demons.

"Why are you invisible?" I ask Dante, my heart pounding as his other hand snakes across my belly, and need rises in me, the bond that ties us together winding tighter.

"Because I can tell you need this," he answers.

"Need what? Your dick massaging my back?" I retort, pretending that his erection prodding me through his pants isn't making me want to spin around and take him in my mouth.

His laugh is so low I almost don't hear it. "If that's what it takes." He pauses, and the next time he speaks his voice is softer and more serious. "You need to know that his death wasn't your fault."

I suck in a sharp breath. "What?"

"You know who I'm talking about," he replies. "It's what's holding you back from claiming your mates, isn't it?"

My heart races faster. "You don't know what you're talking about," I whisper back, though the image of Kai's face appears in my mind and sweat beads on my brow.

"I know that if he was your mate, he wouldn't have died," Dante replies, his arms wrapping possessively around me as he pulls me tighter to him. "Fated mates balance each other."

"Well, we couldn't be sure," I defend.

"And what about me?" he asks. "We both know we're fated, so how can I convince you to let me in, princess?" He kisses my shoulder, his lips hot on my skin, and I shudder.

"Your other mates might have fooled themselves into thinking they can resist you," Dante goes on. "But it's only a matter of time. We all need each other. That's the nature of the fated mates bond."

I smirk at the tortured sound in Dante's voice. Dante, the leader of his clan, heartbreaker of Seral. "Are you saying you *need* me, Dante?" I say, coyly.

I expect him to respond with a smart remark, but he brings his lips to the shell of my ear. "*Yes,* princess." The words are a guttural rasp, and my heart stutters.

"You could end up like Kai," I say, uncrossing my arms as my defenses waver. "By being with me, you could end up in the shadow realm."

"I could," he agrees, and I gasp as his tail wraps around my thigh and squeezes. His invisible fingers press against the front of my pants, his thumb hooking into the material below my belly button. "But I won't. You're my *mate,* Blake."

Desire races through me, but to my right, I see a flicker of movement between the trees. I squint, but there's no one there.

"It's not worth the risk," I tell Dante. "Not until I have all my mates here."

His fingers press harder against the front of my pants, and my lips part.

"Give in, princess. I've waited too long for you to realize that you're mine. Let me give you this."

"If you die, it won't help me."

He chuckles. "Then it's a good thing I'm not planning on dying."

His tail tightens on my thigh as his hand slides into the front of my pants, a single finger swiping through my wetness. "Stop," I rasp, but the sensation of him touching me is too good, and my stomach damn near cramps from the sudden rush of pleasure.

"Everythin' all right, gorgeous?" Nate calls out from back at the campfire.

"Fuck," I breathe as Dante adds another finger, swiping along my core. He kisses a path up my neck and behind my ear.

"I bet even from here the shifter can smell how ready you are," Dante says with a slow drawl. "You should tell him to join us."

An image of both Dante and Nate works into my head, and more wetness pools between my thighs. "And have him die as well? I don't think so."

"I'm sure he'd happily take the risk," Dante chuckles darkly. "Do you still want me to stop?" He continues to tease me, circling his fingers around my entrance, and pushing only his fingertips inside me. Touching. Teasing. Testing me.

"No," I say, desperate for more even though I'm annoyed at how out of control he's making me feel.

"Gorgeous?" Behind me, I hear Nate approaching, and I curse. "Are you sure you're all right?" the shifter asks uncertainly.

"Tell me, princess," Dante whispers seductively into my ear, not at all fazed by the shifter who can't see him. "Tell me you want my fingers inside you. Fucking you. *Filling* you."

I whip my head back toward Nate. "Yes, I'm—" I start to answer his question, but Dante must think I'm responding to him, because he pushes a long finger deep inside me.

Holy Lady Fate.

"Fuck. You're so soft," Dante snarls in my ear as he starts working it in and out of me and adds another finger. I'm wound so tight I almost whimper.

"Blake?" Nate prompts. He's still closer to the campfire than he is to me.

"I...I just need some time to myself right now," I rush out, and Nate stops where he is. His brow furrows with confusion, his features tight. Even Prince Callan looks uncomfortable as he stares from where he's still sitting. Right then I thank Lady Fate that they don't know about Dante's power. If they did, they'd probably realize what was happening. Shade stays silent, and I tell myself she's oblivious, too.

"Okay..." Nate says, dragging out the word.

"We'll move on soon," I squeeze out as Dante uses his thumb to massage my clit.

Nate stares at me for a beat longer, but I give him a strained smile and turn from him, facing the park again. For a moment, I'm afraid Nate will come over to talk to me, but Prince Callan makes a snide remark to the shifter, and I listen as Nate moves back and sits down.

Thank the lady. The feeling of relief is fleeting as

Dante pumps his fingers into me, moving his hand faster. "Give in, princess," he begs as his other hand reaches up to squeeze my breast, and I bite my bottom lip hard to stop from moaning as his hard cock prods my back.

I swear I see movement across the park again, but I'm too consumed by the feeling of Dante's hands on me. Of his fingers, *in* me. I know I should force him off. I should stop him, before this gets out of control. The last thing I want is one of my mates ending up dead, but the scent of apricots and cardamon closes in on me, pleasure obliterating all other thoughts from my mind. I squeeze my eyes shut, biting my bottom lip so hard that I taste blood as I near my release.

"I've got you, princess," Dante whispers, his voice softer than before, and there's something about his tone. Something in the way he says it that has familiarity tickling the back of my mind.

"What?" I ask, my eyes snapping open. "What did you just say?" But he starts rubbing my clit with his thumb again, and I can't stop myself. I fall over the edge, shattering in his hold as pleasure rips through me. Blinding, delicious, pleasure. But the moment the feeling starts to fade, I stiffen. Jerking my head down, fear makes my heart stutter as I stare at my arms, but there aren't any golden marks like when I was with Kai.

Dante is still behind me, and my heart thrashes in my chest. "Dante," I hiss, "I swear if you're dead—"

There's a beat of silence, but then Dante's voice is

in my ear. "You'd what? Scour the shadow realm to find me?"

I clench my teeth to stop the noise of relief that threatens to slip out. *Alive. He's alive.*

We both know once someone's soul enters the shadow realm, there's no way to return to the realms of the living. "I'd have to find a way to save you, just so I could kill you again myself," I croak.

He lets out a barely audible laugh and kisses my cheek. "I don't doubt that." He removes his hand from my pants, but he doesn't let go of me. "One of these nights you're going to let me in completely, princess. I'm not afraid of you."

I check my arms again to make sure they're still bare. "Maybe you should be."

But he keeps holding me, like he's never planning on letting me go.

~ Princess Blake ~

It's not until Nate starts to make his way over again that Dante finally steps away. He reappears back at the campfire shortly after, visible, and with the biggest grin on his face, and I'm pretty sure the shifter and archangel quickly figure out what power the demon has. Neither of them comment, but the pair of them are extra irritable when we leave the demons and head back into the city streets.

Dante stays close to me as we walk, but I'm distracted as I stare at the surrounding buildings. Every so often, I detect the faint scent of chocolate, and I peer at the empty houses half expecting to find the Drozac assassin watching me, but all I see is shadows.

Nate prowls up on my other side. "Four mates are plenty to keep you busy, don't you think, gorgeous?"

I know what he's really asking. Have I found all my mates?

Another waft of chocolate reaches my nose, and I jerk my attention to a rundown building on my right that's leaning to one side. Again, the only thing waiting for me is shadows, and I frown. "I don't know...maybe?" Before we'd found Dante, I was so sure I had more mates out there, but now all I can think about is the fact that the assassin still hasn't joined our group. The next logical thing to do is for us to all try and bond, and after my recent encounter with Dante, I'm feeling more hopeful that my mates will survive it. But going by Prince Callan's hard expression, I don't think he's come around to the idea of bonding just yet.

I'm still trying to decide whether I think I *have* found all my mates when a pool of darkness falls over us. I stop walking and crane my neck, peering up at the ancient temple now towering above us. The structure is crafted from white marble, its thick pillars charred and marked but still standing strong.

"Do you think King Dalton has left a nasty surprise in there?" Shade asks, hopping from one foot to the other on my shoulder.

"Dad wouldn't have defiled their temple," I reply,

and it's not until Nate looks at me strangely that I realize I've spoken out loud.

I clear my throat. "King Dalton might be ruthless, but he wouldn't dishonor a sacred space. This is probably one of the few places we can be sure he hasn't touched."

"Well, that's comfortin'" Nate responds sarcastically.

Ignoring him, I make my way up the cracked stone steps, striding between the central pillars and moving inside the structure. My mates follow behind me, and my eyes widen as I take in the concave ceiling high above us. Whatever used to be painted there looks as if it has been scratched off with giant claws, the deep marks digging into the marble. In the left corner, I spot a small blue eye that was somehow missed.

"Well, that's...unusual," Prince Callan comments as he strolls past me, moving to one of the eight pedestals around the temple. A metal plaque with strange symbols is fixed to each base, but the writing is undecipherable. Piled above the pedestals are handfuls of black stones. There's nothing else in the temple, and I walk closer to another one of the pedestals.

"Do you think these were for their eight gods?" I ask, eyeing the pedestal that's cracked down the center almost as if it has been struck by lightning.

Nate searches the temple like he's hunting for treasure, his keen gaze taking everything in.

"Or eight kings and queens," Prince Callan suggests.

I think about the temples we have back in Seral. They're built to honor Lady Fate, but I know the giants of Rostof worship their royals as if they're gods.

"Maybe they worshipped animals?" Shade adds. *"Just like the Egyptians worshipped cats."*

"Wait, they thought cats were gods?" I say aloud in confusion.

Prince Callan stares at me blankly. "What?"

"Oh, I was just thinking about something. I, uh, once read about humans worshipping cats. It's nothing," I blurt out.

"No, no, I like where this is goin'," Nate says with a grin from a few paces away. Lifting his chin, he puffs out his chest like he's imagining a statue of himself on one of the pedestals.

I roll my eyes. "Yeah, I don't think the humans worshipped cat shifters," I point out.

He shrugs. "What's the difference?"

"Animals don't talk as much, for one," Prince Callan drawls. "Even Toralyn has domesticated cats, and I can attest that they're far more agreeable to be around than shifters."

Dante smirks, and I get the feeling he's enjoying the strange dynamic between us way too much.

"Either way," I say, "I think we can agree something terrible happened here." I peer back at the scratched ceiling, and a heaviness settles onto my shoulders. *"Shade, Seral could have been like this."*

She tucks her wings in tighter. *"Why would the witches defile the temples if they were only after power?"*

"No one knows what fully motivated the witches. For a long time, I thought we'd never find the truth, but now that we know some of the witches survived, maybe one day we'll get to the bottom of it." Stepping forward, I move closer to a pile of the black stones that are sitting atop one of the pedestals. A tiny patch of white is showing on one of them, and I pick up the stone and rub it with my thumb. To my surprise, the black smooths away revealing a glittering white crystal that sparkles and shines, resembling the stones we've seen embedded in the paintings around the city. Flecks of color appear in bursts, and I bring the crystal closer to my face.

Dante's keen gaze is on me, but he doesn't move from where he's leaning against a pillar, watching silently.

"What is that?" Nate asks. Leaning down, he picks up a crystal from the same pile. Like the one I'm holding, it gleams when he cleans away the layer of black, and his gaze lights with curiosity.

"I think I'll keep this for now. For, uh, studyin' later," he mutters and slides the crystal into his pocket.

I stare at the small bulge. "You're going to steal from a temple?"

"Think of it as borrowin'," he replies. "Who knows. You might thank me later."

I give him an exasperated look. "If you say so."

It's daylight when we leave the temple, the weak sunlight streaming through the layer of clouds above and shining on the surrounding buildings. Aside from the crystals, there wasn't anything in the temple to explain what had happened there, and I make a mental note to check it out again once this is all over and I return with my exploration party.

Prince Callan steps up to my side. "It's too quiet," he comments, his alert gaze scanning the street ahead. "By now I would have expected to find more alphas wandering the city confused and starved."

"Or dead," Nate adds.

Dante's brows lower. "The other alphas didn't get their hands on provisions?"

"You say that like you haven't seen anyone else for days," Prince Callan comments.

The demon shrugs. "The group of us woke up not far from each other around the park. Once we defeated the monsters at the fountains, well," he smirks, "you saw what happened."

"We saw somethin' that's for sure," Nate mutters.

I frown at the empty buildings around us. Prince Callan isn't wrong. There were hundreds of alphas at the ball, but we've hardly seen anyone. I stop walking, and my mates halt as well, each of them staring at me.

"I think we should head for the castle," I say abruptly.

Nate raises a brow. "The castle?"

"It should only take the rest of the day to walk there," I go on as I peer up at the ancient castle in the distance. Built atop a large hill in the north of the city, the crumbling towers of the castle are visible above the surrounding buildings, the blackened spires tall and imposing. It was probably magnificent once, a gigantic structure of stone and glass, but now it's just as ruined as the rest of the city.

"Every time I've visited Perstalia in the past, King Dalton created a gateway in the castle. That way we could step straight from Seral, and attend whatever conference was being held," I explain. "So, I think it's safe to assume that's where he'll arrive when he comes. Undoubtedly, he would find us no matter where we are in the city, but we may as well start making our way there." I think of the enchanted gold ring that allows Dad to open gateways to different realms. Each of the rulers of the five allied realms own one, and when I ascend the throne, the ring will become mine. "At least when we're back in Seral, the other alphas will be sent home." *If they're alive, that is...*

"I agree with the princess," Prince Callan says. "We may as well head for the castle and see what happens."

"And what if you haven't found all your mates?" Dante questions me, his dark gaze sliding to my face.

"Then we keep searching while we're on the way," I say with a tight smile.

Nate looks thoughtful, and his nostrils flare as he scents the air. "And what about our assassin friend?"

"What about him?" I ask.

Nate stares at me. "He's out there watchin' us. Do you want me to hunt him down?"

My lips quirk into a smile. "Let him follow. He'll come out eventually."

"Yeah, but it doesn't mean he won't try to kill us first," Nate mutters.

"He won't," I counter. "Not now that he knows we're fated." I pause and tap my finger on my lip. "At least...I don't think he would."

When no one else objects, we start moving again, traveling the winding streets. I'm busy staring at a faded painting that's on the road when Nate lifts his arm, stopping me from taking another step.

His body stiffens. "You smell that?"

Lifting my head, I turn my attention to the end of the street. Prince Callan flicks his wrist, sending a gust of wind rushing toward us, and a distinct coppery scent reaches my nose.

"Blood," I say, drawing my sword.

"Freshly spilled," Nate adds, striding ahead of me.

We turn right onto the next street, and I slow my steps when I spot the carnage up ahead.

"I count six bodies," Shade comments grimly as we get closer.

Nate growls, but he doesn't identify any of the shifters, and we keep moving.

There are more bodies down the next street, and my expression hardens when I stop near the bodies of four broken alphas.

"Demons," Dante says, looking over them.

"Look at how their horns have been harvested," I comment to Shade, my heart rate picking up.

"Wait, Blake, you don't think there are witches here, do you?"

My lips press together, and I share a tense look with Dante. We both knew these demons and the clans they belonged to. *Fuck.*

"Guess they didn't make it to that park you were all at," Prince Callan says to Dante.

Nate squats down to check on a body that's crumpled near the side of a building in a pool of blood. "Still warm. Whoever did this, they can't be far."

It's all I need to hear.

Gripping my sword tighter, I flap my wings and launch into the air.

"What are you doing?" Shade asks as she flies from my shoulder, pushed away by the force of the wind.

Dante calls after me, but all I can focus on is the ringing in my ears and my pounding heart. No demon has had their horns harvested since the witches were defeated, and these alphas were here because of me.

Beating my wings, I fly above the houses, scanning the nearby streets. Prince Callan and Shade follow after me, and I hear Nate's roar from somewhere below. Dante is probably not far behind either. A small part of me knows we shouldn't have split up, but I can't let the witches get away. If they're here, I need to keep one alive for questioning, but the rest will die by my blade. They roamed this land once, destroying everything in their path, and I'm not willing to let the demons be next.

I fly faster, the wind whistling in my ears as I frantically search every shadow and movement below, but all I see is more scattered bodies. A trail of dead alphas leads me further into the city, and they're not all demons and shifters. There are archangels and water monsters, too, and I clench my jaw, fury swelling in my chest.

The cool metal of my hilt bites into my palm, and surprise mixes with my anger when I spot three alphas walking the street below. They're not witches. They're *giants*. Blood drips from the two-sided axes resting on their massive shoulders, and the demon horns hanging from their belts. I land silently on the street behind them, and Prince Callan drops down next to me soon after. Shade stays in the air, circling from above like she's letting the others know where we are.

"You sure this is a good idea, Drax?" the voice of one of the giants rumbles down the street. "These are dangerous folk we're messin' with."

There's a grunt of agreement, and another alpha responds. "The demon king likes to play games, but for once, he's gotten more than he bargained for. I'm just glad the tip off we received about the king's plans turned out to be accurate."

Tip off? My blood chills.

"They knew we were going to get sent here," I mutter under my breath in disbelief.

Prince Callan draws his sword, his face a mask of

casual indifference. "How fortunate for them. Now, who gets to take the extra one. You or me?"

I adjust my grip on my sword. Before I can answer, Nate bounds onto the street in his shifted form and pads up beside us. His gaze focuses on the giants up ahead as the three of them turn toward us.

"Well, I guess we get one each then," Prince Callan amends like he's disappointed.

"Ah, Princess Blake, you've finally found us," Drax, the giant in the middle of the trio says. Now that he's facing me, I instantly recognize that he's the same giant Prince Callan toyed with in the ballroom. Drax smiles cruelly when he spots the archangel. "And I see you have company."

"Sorry to keep you waiting," I say, my voice dripping with sarcasm. "Had I known you'd throw a temper tantrum until you had my attention, I'd have come sooner. Though, I must say, if we're fated mates I think I might have to cut out my own eyes."

Drax scowls. "That's big talk for someone in your position."

Prince Callan strokes his chin. "And what position would that be?"

"The position of someone who's about to lose a kingdom and witness the downfall of the demons," the giant on the right laughs, and Drax shoots him a stern look.

Nate starts to pace, and the churning in my stomach intensifies. "What are you talking about?"

Drax's smile grows wider. "Yeah, I suspect you

have no idea what's goin' on, do you, your highness? All you need to know is that you won't need to worry about becomin' queen of Seral. Arrangements 'ave already been made."

The giant on his right laughs again, and as if on cue, the other giant who's been silent this whole time lifts his hand and brings a small, tubed instrument to his mouth. I frown. *No, it's not an instrument...* "Stop!" I shout as Nate and Prince Callan launch forward.

My warning comes too late, and Nate growls as a dart sinks into his chest. Prince Callan deflects a dart aimed at his face, but another strikes his arm.

The wind whips around us as Prince Callan tries to use his power, but it dies off quickly as the archangel staggers and then collapses to the ground. Nate keeps trying to run toward the giants, but his legs buckle and his chin slams to the stones beneath his paws.

I narrow my eyes at the giants, but my vision starts to blur. Peering down, I blink at the dart that's now protruding from my lower leg. I hadn't even felt it.

"I'm coming!" Shade's distressed voice fills my mind, and she swoops down, her claws closing around the small, tubed weapon. Before she can fly off, the giant holding the weapon swats at her. She lets out a pained squawk, and I hear a thud.

"No!" I stumble forward, trying to clear my vision, but I can feel the poison polluting my bloodstream and weakening me. My body tingles as it tries to heal, but it's not fast enough to beat the poison.

"What'd I say?" Drax chuckles to his friends. "It can't get easier than this."

As they stride closer, I prepare myself to fight. Anger flows through me, but I can hardly lift my arms, and the sword slips from my grasp. "What have you done?" I slur as the three giants seem to multiply until there's an army of them in front of me. My teeth begin to chatter, and a blow comes from my left driving me to my knees. For the first time in a long while, fear trickles through me. Fear for Shade. And for my mates.

Before the giant on the right can strike me again, a fist smashes through his ribcage from behind, and splotches of red coat Dante's body. Dante wrenches his arm back out and the giant falls to the ground, but Drax's ax slams into the demon's chest. I don't see what happens next through the spots of black clouding my vision, but I hear Dante's body fall.

"No," I breathe.

"Oh, don't worry, your highness, you won't need them where you're goin'," Drax mocks by my ear, and his stench of rotting flesh makes me gag. Focusing on the sound of his voice, I take a second to judge the distance before smashing my head into his. Pain shoots through my skull, stars bursting behind my eyes, but I smile when he lets out a stream of curses.

"Rostof will pay for this," I tell him, smiling even though I can no longer see at all. "The giants won't get Seral." I knew negotiations between our realms weren't going well, but I hadn't expected them to resort to this.

There's a moment of silence, and then Drax lets out a braying laugh. "What makes you think we're doin' this for the giants?"

My mind spins, and my heart stutters when I remember the horns hanging from their belts. "The witches," I hiss. "Why would you side with them?"

"It was an easy deal to make," he replies smugly. "They care about the power and energy they can take from you demons. They don't care about ruling the kingdom and owning the land."

"So they promised you Seral?" I say like he's an idiot. "And you believed that?"

A fist slams into my jaw, and I spit out the blood pooling in my mouth.

"Good thing they came to me, too," he snarls. "Because right now I'm the only one who has you. You should be thankin' your Lady Fate or whomever your god is that I've been instructed to keep you alive."

I think about the stories I've heard about demons who were captured by the witches and experimented on. From what I've been told, the witches were trying to find a way to harvest our power without having to kill us, but as far as I'm aware no solution was found. *And now they're about to get another test subject.*

"The only one I'll be thanking is myself," I reply dryly. "When I rid us of the witches once and for all."

Drax only laughs again, and the next time a fist smashes against the side of my head, I detect the faint scent of mint and chocolate before I lose myself completely to the darkness.

CHAPTER

TWENTY

~ Alaric ~

Fury consumes me as I let loose multiple arrows in rapid succession. Two of the giants are on the ground within seconds, but Drax is still standing over the demon princess, a single arrow protruding from his shoulder.

I jump down from the roof I'm on and stalk toward the worm of a male not far from me. To his credit, he doesn't try to run when he sees the tattoos covering my arms.

"Drozac," he says with a strained smile. "How nice of you to join me. I gather she must be your—"

"Target," I finish for him.

"Ah yes," he says, "but you see, the thing is she's promised to someone else."

219

I crack my knuckles. "The code is clear. A Drozac never fails to take out their target."

He holds my stare, and I adjust my grip on the hilt of my sword.

I'm not surprised when he concedes. "Then I guess I'll have to explain her death," he says with a toothy smile. He peers down at the princess, and his grin grows bigger. "Promise me you'll make her suffer. The stupid bitch—"

He doesn't finish. I'd intended to question him more, but my blade is through his neck and silencing him before he can utter another word. It's a quicker death than he deserved, but he's not my priority right now.

Turning, I peer down at the unconscious female on the ground. Her long black hair is soaked with blood, but the gash I'd seen open up on her forehead has already healed.

Blood drips from my sword. She's the reason I'm here. My target. My purpose. Another name to add to the long list of lives I've taken as a member of the Drozac. She's my revenge for my brother's death, and the key to taking down King Dalton. Decades, I've waited for this. I told myself I couldn't let Drax have her. The giant had lost his way if he'd sided with the witches, but that wasn't it. Watching him strike her had blinding anger rolling through me.

My fingers twitch on the hilt of my sword. *You're my mate.* Her words fill my head. She has to be wrong, but the wind stirs, tunnelling down the street, and I brace as her scent hits me. The alluring smell of honey and cinnamon threatens to cripple my resolve, and I clench my jaw.

I stare at her pink cheeks and dark lashes. Her feathered wings are splayed behind her, and she looks more like an avenging angel than a demon princess. An image of her face contorted with ecstasy as I watched the invisible demon pleasure her at the park fills my mind, and my cock instantly hardens.

Control yourself, Alaric, I tell myself. Whatever response my body is having, it must be wrong. The female is my enemy, a royal of Seral, and the price that must be paid for the death of my brother. I grind my teeth. Decades I've waited for this moment. For this one chance to make things right.

I lift my blade. A single strike. That's all it would take. Mentally, I fight against her scent. Against the allure of the demon. If I'm wrong and she is my mate, I'll feel this for eternity. The mistake won't just haunt me, it will terrorize me. But I've endured years of pain, and I'm not afraid to endure more.

My hand shakes. *A target. That's all she is.* But one of her mates starts to stir behind me, and I act on instinct. Sheathing my sword, I scoop the princess into my arms and carry her away.

TWENTY-ONE

~ Nate ~

Princess Blake is gone when I lift to my feet, and panic makes my muscles tighten. The three giants are dead on the ground, their bodies still warm and the scent of their blood strong in the air. I scowl, wishing I had been the one to end them. That I could have been the one watching as the life drained from their eyes.

"Blake!" Dante shouts, and I turn my attention to the demon who's scanning the street. He's holding one of the giant's axes, and his dark eyes blaze with anger.

"How long were we out?" Prince Callan asks coldly as he rises to his feet.

"It's hard to tell," I bite out, moving to stand over

one of the giants, "but goin' by the bodies, I'd guess not long."

Prince Callan comes up beside me and stares at the multiple arrows protruding from the giants' bodies. "The princess didn't do this."

"You think it was the assassin?" Dante asks, his gaze still searching the surrounding buildings. "The one she believes is her mate?"

Prince Callan looks uncertain. "I've never heard of a Drozac assassin having a mate."

The demon frowns. "So, you think she was wrong about him?"

Prince Callan flicks his wrist using wind magic to retrieve his discarded sword. "Who can say."

Fuck, I want to make someone bleed. I clench and unclench my fists. Stepping a few paces away, adrenaline courses through my body as I shift, taking on my beast form. A roar rips from me the moment the change is complete, making the stones vibrate under my paws. Dropping my nose to the street, I breathe in, searching for Blake's scent. *My mate. My queen.* It doesn't take long for me to detect her, and I don't spare the others another glance as I leap forward, picking up speed as I run between the buildings.

"He's found her!" Prince Callan shouts behind me and he takes to the sky, following me from above. Dante isn't far behind, his boots pounding the pavement, and it's not until Shade squawks that I tip my head up, taking note of where she's appeared. She flaps her wings furiously, desperately trying to keep up with the prince.

Right now, I can't think about them. All I can think about is the fact that someone's taken my mate from me. I push myself harder, and the buildings become a blur as my powerful body takes me further into the city.

It feels like hardly any time has passed when Blake's scent leads me to a three-story structure with a flat roof. I don't slow my pace as I leap onto the side of the building, my claws digging in as I climb the stone walls and head for one of the higher windows. Dante jumps up beside me, grunting as his fingers dig into the grooves between the stones, and the steady flapping of wings tells me Callan is descending from above.

My blood pounds faster as Blake's scent grows stronger, and a protective instinct I'd long since thought I'd lost drives me forward, screaming at me to move faster. If the assassin has hurt her, I'll tear him apart.

TWENTY-TWO

~ Princess Blake ~

When I wake, I immediately reach for the curved dagger strapped to my thigh. Rising, I prepare myself to attack the giants who have captured me, but I'm surprised to find the Drozac assassin sitting a short distance away. His gray eyes bore into me as he watches from the corner of the small room we're in. Sweet chocolate and crisp mint swirls in the air, and instinctively my muscles relax, but I don't release my grip on my blade. "Where are we?"

He doesn't answer, and I warily eye the silver cuffs around his wrists. "Tell me where we are, *mate*," I bite out.

He bristles, his top lip curling. "You're safe. For now," he replies gruffly. His voice is so rough and deep it crackles when he speaks, and my heart rate picks up as I fight against the desire to move closer to him.

"And the others?" I ask, my throat tight.

His expression gives nothing away, but after a long moment he answers. "I imagine the shifter, demon, and archangel will be here soon."

My chest sags. Inside, I knew they weren't dead. I would feel pain if they'd been killed and their souls sent to the shadow realm, but it's a relief to know they haven't been captured. At that, my mind whirls as I think about the witches, but I mentally push my questions away. There would be time to figure out that puzzle, but for now, I have to deal with my current situation.

Scanning the room, I take note of the neatly ordered provisions, the weapons lined against the wall, and the assassin's cloak spread on the floor. *He's taken me to where he's been staying?* My gaze lifts again. "Either hurry up and kill me already or tell me where the giants are." Anger races through me at the thought of the giants we encountered, and I tighten my grip on my blade. I wouldn't be so careless around those traitors again.

My fury is mirrored in the assassin's eyes, and his jaw clenches. "They're not here. They touched you," he rasps like that one statement explains everything.

I jerk my chin higher, even though my heart

skitters at his words. "And what? They weren't killing me fast enough for your liking?"

He blinks slowly, and his nostrils flare. "They weren't killing you because their heads were rolling on the ground before they could draw another breath."

My heart pounds faster. "Saving me for yourself, were you?"

His eyes darken, heat entering his gaze, and I swallow hard.

"You saved me because you're my mate, and you know it," I say when he doesn't speak. The words come out breathier than I intend, and his scent of mint and chocolate grows stronger, making my body ache. I definitely did something to offend Lady Fate considering where I am now.

I'm distracted enough that I'm slow to react when the assassin launches across the room. He slams my back against the wall, and my dagger flies from my grip. *Oh, shit.* The air rushes from my lungs, and his hands wrap around my wrists as he holds them above my head and pins me there. "Drozac assassins don't have mates," he snarls, and his dark brown hair hangs around his face as he leans in close.

Heat races through my veins, and my breath hitches as his intense gray gaze lowers to my lips. "That's funny," I tell him, "because *you* do."

He sucks in a sharp breath, flinching like I've struck him, but instead of moving away, he presses in closer.

"You don't understand, as a member of the Drozac,

I took an oath," he says, his lips dangerously close to mine. "Whatever this is, it's a mistake. I *can't* have a mate. I can't have anyone."

My brows lift, and I stare at him in surprise. "Well, maybe you said the oath wrong." I pause thoughtfully. "Wait, are you saying you haven't been with anyone since you made your oath? How long ago was that?"

His jaw clenches.

"Well, shit. No wonder you're so grumpy."

The thick muscles across his chest tighten, and I tense. "If you were going to kill me, you wouldn't have saved me from your pals out there."

"Maybe I just want you to suffer first," he replies gruffly, tightening his hold on my wrists.

I think his idea is to intimidate me, but all it's doing is turning me on even more. I'm guessing he must feel the same way, because he presses his hips against me, and strain pulls across his features.

I smirk. "Give it up, assassin. Because whether we like it or not, Lady Fate has plans for us."

He breathes heavily. "I was sent here to take your life."

"Yes, well, it's the giants who are being difficult with the negotiations. Instead of sending you to do their dirty work, maybe the royals of Rostof should get their heads out of their asses and actually have a realistic conversation with King Dalton. I mean, don't you ever say 'no' to them?"

He frowns at me like I'm speaking gibberish. "No."

I smile sweetly. "Then I guess there's a first time for everything."

"You're the demon princess," he whispers like saying it out loud is blasphemy.

"And you're an asshole," I reply. "So it looks like we both lucked ou—"

Before I can finish, he smashes his lips to mine, and the kiss is rough and possessive, and it sets my body on fire. Cool mint and chocolate fills my mouth, sweet and bitter, and mouthwateringly delicious as his tongue pushes in, stroking and demanding that I respond. His hips press harder against me, and every other thought empties from my mind, replaced by the desire to have more of him. Need races through me. A need so strong it's almost painful. I *need* him.

Using my power, I yank my hands free and push him with enough force that he falls with his back flat to the floor. Before he can get up, I'm on him, my knees sliding to the sides of his hips as lust wars with the hatred in his cool and calculating gray eyes. He's so big between my legs, and I enjoy the feel of him beneath me. His large hands reach behind my back, and when I grind against him, the growl that comes from him is a feral, guttural sound that turns my insides to liquid.

"Demon enchantress," he curses as he peers up at me, and there's a tortured look in his eyes. "After all these years, this is a test to finally break me."

I can't blame him for believing that. He's right about this not making any sense. If he wasn't my mate, I would kill him in a heartbeat and I'd enjoy it, too. But he is, and I rock against him as I arch my back, enjoying the hard press of him between my thighs. When I look down, the hate is gone from his eyes, the emotion drowned by a desire so intense, all I can think about is having him inside me. Filling me and riding me until I'm too exhausted to move.

Before I can think about giving in and wrestling the assassin out of his clothes, he curses and breaks his hands free from my hold. His grip tightens on my back, and he rolls us to the side right before Prince Callan crashes through the ceiling. Debris and dust shower around us, and Nate climbs through the window in his shifted form, followed by Dante who wields a giant ax. Shade is the last to enter, and she soars straight for the assassin, pecking at his face furiously as she frantically flaps her wings. He lifts his hand to protect his eyes and grumbles another curse, but he doesn't harm her.

"Shade, stop!" I send to her, but she keeps going.

"Tell me you're all right!" she squawks in my mind, and my heart clenches at the panic in her voice.

"The assassin saved me," I tell her quickly, trying to ease her worry. *"And as much as I appreciate the support, you can stop attacking my mate now."*

She pecks him a few more times before flying to the closest windowsill and tucking in her wings. Her feathers are still ruffled as she paces. *"Well, you'd better tell that to these three before things get out of hand."*

I lift to my feet, facing the glowering males who are positioned around the room, and the assassin does the same. Dante's face is the picture of wrath as his tail flicks and he stares down the Drozac, and Nate roars, his mouth stretching wide as he bares his fangs like he's imagining crushing the assassin's head. Prince Callan's normally perfectly smoothed hair is tousled and unruly, and stress lines are tight across his face.

My lips curve into a smile. "Aw, you guys care about me," I croon happily. Either that, or they simply care about keeping me alive, but I let myself believe the first option.

Dante's chest heaves up and down, and he assesses the way I'm instinctively standing in front of the assassin. Slowly, the anger in his eyes starts to dissipate. "So, I'm guessing this is the other mate you were telling me about?" he says coolly, though there's still a deranged look in his eyes that's making me feel all hot and bothered. Then again, that might be because my mates are around me all looking incredibly delectable right now. Or maybe, it's because we almost just died, and I'm so damn relieved to see them alive.

"Yup," I say with a ridiculously giddy smile.

"The Drozac assassin," Prince Callan says with disgust, but the assassin doesn't look the least bit affronted by the contempt in the archangel's voice.

"He saved me from the giants," I say, and it feels weird to be defending a member of the Drozac. "I mean, I would have just killed them when I woke, but uh, thanks," I add, turning to the assassin. Despite his relaxed stance, his alert gaze doesn't shift from my mates.

When the others keep acting hostile, I shoot them a stern look until one by one they slowly lower their weapons. Nate hisses and paces before changing back to his non-shifted form, his body molding and changing, and the thick spotted fur disappearing.

Behind me, the assassin's brows lower as he watches them follow my command. "Guess I'm not the only one who's lost my mind," he comments. "They act like your pets, just like your bird." He gestures with his head to Shade.

I stiffen. *Oh boy.* There really is only so much you can do to help a guy out.

*"Tell me he did **not** just say that!"* Shade screeches as she shoots forward, her claws outstretched as she aims for his face.

His eyes widen in surprise, and he dodges, avoiding her attacks.

"You shouldn't have called her that," I point out with a grin.

"What?" he grunts, looking genuinely puzzled as Shade continues to squawk at him.

"You called her a pet," I explain. "When I found her, she'd been locked in a cage and was half dead. She knows that word and she's not exactly a fan."

"Well, I'm glad he's the one to find that out," Prince Callan says with amusement.

The assassin processes my words, and to my surprise, his expression softens. It's not sympathy I detect, but maybe...understanding? When Shade flies at him again, he lifts his hands in a placating gesture.

"Stop, little one. I didn't mean to offend you, and something tells me I'd regret having to break your neck."

Shade squawks and retreats back to the windowsill, and I glare at him. "Do that, and even if you are my mate I will happily send you to the shadow realm."

Dante folds his arms across his chest, and his lips twitch. "And here I thought I had a way with words."

The assassin scowls.

"So, what's the plan here?" Nate says, folding his arms behind his head and widening his stance. The naked male has a raging hard on, and I can't even tell him to put his clothes back on because I'm guessing he probably shredded them when he shifted again.

All gazes turn to me, and for a moment, I don't know what to say. Their scents are all mixing together, and it's messing with my head. *Stupid fated mates.* "We need to find out what's going on with the witches," I say, blurting the first coherent thought that comes to me.

I'm aware that the assassin might know what the giants were up to, though I doubt he is involved. It's well known the Drozac assassins try to keep out of the everyday workings of society. Their oath is to their order.

"I meant, what are you doin' with the four of us?" Nate clarifies, giving me a wolfish grin.

I hesitate. The obvious answer is that we bond now to find out if they're all my mates, but Prince

Callan has made it clear he's not willing to participate, and I doubt the assassin will be happy to join just yet, either.

"We go back to the plan of making our way to the castle," I suggest. "It's our way home, and if the witches have infiltrated Rostof, we need to get word to King Dalton. Then we can worry about what to do with..." I gesture to the four males around me, "uh, this."

When no one argues, I call it a win and stride toward the doorway. Shade flies over, perching on my shoulder, and I make it a few steps into the hallway before I realize no one else is following us. Peering back, I sigh when I find that Dante, Prince Callan, and Nate are all still glaring at the assassin.

"You first, Drozac," Prince Callan says coldly.

The assassin collects his weapons and provisions from the floor and slings a leather satchel over his shoulder. "It's Alaric," he says, striding after me and ducking to fit through the doorway. "And you're welcome."

The others grumble as they follow, and it's tense as we make our way from the house.

"Great," I say to Shade. *"This is just great."*

TWENTY-THREE

~ Princess Blake ~

It takes the rest of the day, and part of the night for us to reach the moat that stretches around the castle, and we stop a short distance away. The drawbridge is down but considering the smeared blood and marks on the aged wood, I'm guessing there's something in the wide stretch of still black water that surrounds the castle walls. *Of course, there is.*

"Whoa, we're not walking across that are we?" Shade asks.

I stretch my wings. *"Don't worry. We can fly, remember?"*

She sighs in my head, and I turn to face the guys. I get the feeling that none of them are overly keen about being here, but no one's complaining. Not even Alaric, who I had thought would have changed his mind by now. I guess when it comes down to it, we all know this is the fastest way for us to get out of Perstalia.

"So, I think it's safe to assume that the bridge is a death trap," I point out, hooking my thumb over my shoulder to indicate to the drawbridge. "But, luckily, some of us have wings, so we can carry you across and set down inside the walls."

"I'm not being carried like an infant," Alaric grumbles.

I plant a hand on my hip. The urge to tell him to stay behind is on the tip of my tongue, but without him, we can't seal the fated mates bond. Without him, I won't be able to unlock my power. It's bad enough that Prince Callan is still resistant to the idea, but I thought I'd gotten through to the assassin. Our fates are entwined, whether he likes it or not.

Nate crosses his arms. The shifter is wearing the clothes of a dead alpha we passed on our way here, and it's strange seeing him without his midriff showing. He tips his head toward Alaric. "I'm with him. Cats aren't meant to fly." His gaze slides to Prince Callan. "Besides, I'm not puttin' my life in his hands."

Prince Callan's eyes darken. "Now, I think that's the smartest thing you've said so far."

I roll my eyes and turn my attention to where Dante has been silently observing us. "And what about you? Anything you want to complain about?"

His dark eyes glimmer with amusement, and he

taps his chin with his finger, his expression becoming thoughtful. "Mmmm, no I'm more than happy to be air lifted over these walls if it means lessening the time until I'm between your thighs."

My cheeks heat, my body warming at the thought of him between my legs again, and the other guys glare at him.

"Oh, now that's a reply worthy of a fated mate," Shade swoons.

"What?" Dante says to the others with a devilish smirk. "Some of you might have convinced yourselves you don't want this, but I've tasted my princess, and I'll happily spend my life making her scream my name."

"Fucking demons," Alaric growls and drops the leather satchel he's been holding before pulling out the two swords at his sides. Cracking his neck, he doesn't even spare me another glance before he strides forward and steps out onto the bridge.

I don't try to stop him. If he's not willing to be carried, this is the only way across. Still, my breath catches in my throat as I watch him take one step after the other. He moves carefully, his gaze sharp and alert, and his steps light despite his large size.

"Bastard has balls," Dante comments.

Nate only waits a moment before he starts stripping off his clothes. When he's fully naked, he winks at me. "When it's my turn with you, I'll make sure you forget his name and only remember mine. See you on the other side, gorgeous."

Dante smirks wickedly. "Something tells me she'll want to forget more than that when she's with you."

Shade's laughter fills my head, and Nate glowers at the demon before turning to Prince Callan. "Here hang on to these, will ya," he says and shoves his clothes into the prince's hands. Before Prince Callan can complain, Nate's body is shifting until he's a giant cat again.

Prince Callan narrows his eyes as Nate nudges me with his nose, and my face flushes as a deep rumbling sound vibrates in the cat's chest. Then Nate turns from me and starts crossing the bridge, his paws silent on the decayed wood. His long strides bring him closer to where Alaric is already halfway across, and for a moment, I think nothing bad is going to happen. That is, until the black water starts bubbling, and something large moves under the surface. *Ah, fuck.*

"I do hope you weren't expecting them to live," Prince Callan says unhelpfully as he drops Nate's clothes, letting them fall to the ground.

"They aren't just my mates," I point out as I pick up the clothes and bundle them in my arms. "You're bound to them too, and if they die, we all lose."

Dante mutters a curse like he'd been purposely trying to forget that part, and he reaches for his sword at the same time as I do.

The bubbles reach the bridge, and I launch into the air as four giant tentacles spear from the water, rising up on either side of the bridge. "Run!" I yell at Alaric and Nate.

Alaric slices through a massive, wet tentacle aimed for him, leaps over another one, and rolls before cleaving into a third tentacle that swipes toward him. Nate roars and slashes at a tentacle with his front paws, but one of the other tentacles moves away from Alaric and goes for the shifter, wrapping around my mate's torso and lifting him high into the air. My heart lurches as he struggles and the tentacle rushes downward, smashing the shifter's body against the bridge. Nate roars again, his fangs sinking into blubbery flesh as he's lifted back into the air. The tentacle swings from side to side, but it doesn't loosen.

Two of the other tentacles rush at Alaric again, and he dodges away from one, only to be picked up by the other.

"No!" Shade laments in my head. *"Tentacles aren't meant to be scary! Books have taught me they're for good times!"*

I have no idea what she's on about, and I don't ask as I rush toward the monster with my sword brandished before me. Swooping down, I slice through the massive tentacle holding Nate, severing the circular suckers as I cut clean through the flesh. The detached tentacle loosens as it falls, and Nate jumps back to the bridge, landing on his feet. Something screams below the water, and huge bubbles rise to the surface as the water ripples.

Using his blade, Alaric cuts himself free, but another tentacle is quick to wrap around him. It winds around his body, pinning his arms to his sides, and he shouts something that I can't hear over the din of the creature's cries.

Four more tentacles spring from the water as Prince Callan launches into the sky, flying lower toward Alaric. Two tentacles go for the archangel, and he uses wind power to batter away a tentacle that rushes his right side. The tentacle rears back in the air, but another comes from behind and slams into him with enough force that it sends him careening downward. *Dammit.* I angle down to try and catch him, but the prince flaps his wings, steadying himself and rising just before he hits the black water.

"*Blake!*" Shade's shrill warning is in my head as she flaps high above me, not willing to get close to the monster. I turn to see Alaric's still struggling against the tightening hold of a tentacle, his face reddening. Nate is pacing at the other end of the bridge, but he doesn't move to help.

"*What the fuck? Does he not get that if one of us dies, it'll suck for all of us?*"

I pivot, soaring toward Alaric with my sword, and this time it's Dante who bellows a warning right before the water explodes. A wave of water sprays into the air as the head of the massive monster rises from the moat, huge milky white eyes fixing on us as its massive maw opens revealing a set of razor-sharp teeth.

Merciful Lady Fate, the creature is large enough it could swallow us all whole.

The monster drags the tentacle holding Alaric

closer to its fanged mouth, and I beat my wings harder as my heart pounds in my ears. Alaric snarls, trying to twist and wiggle himself free, but it's not helping.

A tentacle flies toward me, and I maneuver in the air, lashing out with my blade. This only angers the creature, and two more tentacles aim for me. One wraps around my legs, and Nate's roar comes to me from across the bridge.

Alaric is pulled closer to the creature's jaws, and I watch in horror as my fated mate is powerless to stop it. I slice against the tentacle holding me, but as soon as it falls away another one wraps around my waist, while another binds my legs again. Nate's clothes slip from my arms, and I'm dragged downward, but a floating blade severs one of the tentacles from below. Green ichor sprays onto Dante's invisible body, coating enough of him that I can make out an outline.

Nate races across the bridge and leaps, clawing and chomping on the other tentacle until I'm freed, but more tentacles appear, binding me.

Dante and Nate work to try and free me, but I shout, telling them to get Alaric. Prince Callan flies toward the assassin again as the male's feet near the creature's gigantic tongue, and Alaric's gaze connects with mine. There's a flicker of hatred in his eyes, but then the tentacles around me squeeze tighter, and I cry out as some of my ribs snap. Alaric growls, his eyes igniting with fury, and then his body grows, rapidly increasing in size. The tentacles are forced to release him as his limbs grow larger, and the male turns into a massive giant. Standing tall, he becomes the height of the castle walls, and he grabs onto the tentacles that are holding me and he squeezes until the blubbery flesh explodes, ichor spurting onto his thick arms.

Freed, I flap my wings, catching myself before I fall, and the sea creature omits a sound that makes my ears bleed. Prince Callan shouts something and lifts his hands. Using his magic, he creates a wind tunnel to surround the beast, absorbing the sound. It must amplify the noise for the beast, as the creature thrashes, its bloodied tentacles swiping wildly through the air. Alaric snarls as he punches the creature, sending the beast flying backward into the water, and the world grows quiet as the creature disappears below the surface.

None of us waste time. I fly to the other end of the drawbridge and as soon as we're all across, Alaric reaches for the iron crank system. The rusted chains rattle as he lifts the drawbridge, sealing us within the castle walls.

Shade flies down, letting out a stream of panicked comments in my head before settling on my shoulder. Nate shifts back, standing there completely naked, and Dante turns visible again, his clothes coated with green ichor. Prince Callan smooths his hair looking way too relaxed, and Alaric returns to his smaller form. The silver cuffs are no longer on his wrists, and I let out a shaky breath.

"Well, that was a shit show," I say, because if it

wasn't for Alaric, who knows what might have happened.

"That wasn't just a monster," Prince Callan discusses calmly. "That was one of the deadliest sea beasts from Norso. They have powerful natural healing abilities, and it won't be long until the creature is back to its full strength."

Alaric nods, agreeing with the archangel's statement.

"When we're back in Seral and this is over, I'll organize for the creature to be returned home," I say. "King Dalton must have bribed some natives from Norso to help transfer it here. It shouldn't be too hard to find out who they are."

"Blake, it looks like we're not the only ones who made it," Shade says grimly, and I turn, my lips thinning when I take note of the three alphas around the bailey —the open area that's like a courtyard stretching around the castle. Two of the alphas are missing limbs and lying in pools of blood, but the third is propped up against the castle wall.

"This one's still alive," Nate says, inspecting the third alpha. I move closer to see the shifter is breathing harshly. The male's eyes are closed, and it'll take a good while for the wound on his chest to heal, but he'll be fine.

"Should you check to see if he's your mate?" Nate says, grabbing the alpha and bringing him closer to me. The male's head lolls to the side, and I make a face.

"Don't do that," I chastise.

"Do what?" Nate asks, holding out the shifter like he's expecting me to take a whiff.

"*That,*" I say, indicating to the poor male who doesn't realize he's being manhandled. "He's not my mate." I could tell from the moment I moved close to him.

"Okay, if you say so," Nate says and drops the shifter with a thud to the ground. Then he starts stripping off the guy's shirt.

"What are you doing?" I hiss.

"Well, I'm not goin' to wear their clothes, now am I?" he defends, gesturing with his head to the other two mutilated alphas whose clothes are torn and bloody. "And seein' as the archangel couldn't handle the simple task of bringin' the outfit I was wearin' before, this'll have to do."

I roll my eyes, but I don't point out that I was the one who dropped his clothes into the water. When Nate's finished dressing, I groan and prop the unconscious alpha back against the wall, because the poor guy has clearly been through enough already. As I go to step back, I freeze. A short distance away, another one of my black feathers lies discarded on the stones, and my heart skips a beat. It's the third I've lost since we've been in Perstalia, and I can't shake the sense of foreboding creeping over me.

Alaric watches me carefully, but he doesn't say anything.

When Nate finishes tying the straps on his new

pants he grins. "All right then, who's ready to head back to Seral?"

I clear my throat. "We have to survive the castle first," I point out, striding away from the feather, and peering up at the giant structure looming over us. Despite the worn stone, the tall white towers gleam in the watery moonlight that streams through the clouds above, and crystals sparkle in the crevices between the bricks. The last time I was here, I couldn't stop marveling at the place, but now just the sight of it fills me with dread. Mentally, I run through the different kinds of monsters Dad might have lured inside. Truthfully, he would have chosen monsters that tested anyone who entered, but now that I'm standing before the castle, I'm almost certain he expected me to come here. Just as I'm certain there's something nasty planted inside especially for me.

Pivoting, I smack my lips together and address my mates. "All right, I think we all know we're not going to survive this unless we work together, so I think it's time to set down some ground rules."

They all look at me as if I'm overreacting, but no one protests, so I forge on. I hold up a finger. "Rule number one: Don't get separated. Inside, it's a maze of rooms and corridors, and I don't want to have to go searching when you end up somewhere you don't want to be." I pace and hold up another finger. "Rule number two: Don't touch anything. To this day, no one has explored all of the rooms in the castle because of the suspected ancient booby traps that haven't been activated."

"Traps? What kind of castle is this?" Nate grumbles.

Prince Callan smirks. "Concerned, Nine Lives?"

Nate's slitted gaze shifts to the archangel. "Curious."

Ignoring them, I continue on, holding up a third finger. "Rule number three: Work on keeping each other alive. You don't have to like each other, but if anyone dies, we're all affected, so get your heads out of your asses and don't just stand there if someone's about to be eaten." I glare at Nate now, but he only gives me a shit-eating grin.

"Lastly," I say, lifting a fourth finger, "rule number four: Don't die." You'd think I wouldn't have to make this point, but considering the fiasco on the bridge, I'm starting to wonder about some of my mates.

"I hate to break it to you, but I don't think they're listening," Shade says sympathetically as Prince Callan makes a snide remark about Nate not deserving to live, and the shifter shoots back a retort. I sigh and turn to the door at the base of the castle. If I were alone, I'd fly around the building and enter through one of the tower windows, but that's not happening. *Yay,* I think sarcastically. *Looks like we're going through the front door.*

TWENTY-FOUR

~ Princess Blake ~

Surprisingly, there isn't anything bad waiting for us on the other side of the door. We make our way into the castle and up a series of corridors without incident, and it's not until we reach a main corridor on the fourth floor that I take note of the hidden panels on the walls. Before we enter, I toss a discarded piece of broken wood into the air ahead of us, and jets of fire explode in the corridor, blocking the way ahead. *Shit.*

"Can't say I'm in the mood to be roasted," Prince Callan comments, studying the fire. "What now?"

"Now, we wait," I instruct. I've always known about the booby trap in this corridor, but it's usually deactivated. I concentrate on counting the streams of fire and tossing more pieces of discarded wood into the corridor when the jets stop. It takes me a good while to memorize the pattern and figure out a path through, but eventually I think I'm ready.

Lifting my hand, I point to a small metal lever against the wall on the opposite end of the corridor. "I'll go first and turn it off so you guys can come across."

Dante's brows slam down. "Let me do it."

I shake my head. "I've grown up dealing with tests like this. Besides, I'm smaller so it's easier for me to avoid the fire." He still looks unhappy at the idea of me going first, but he steps back giving me space. Taking a deep breath, I wait until the fire stops yet again, and I launch into the corridor, counting in my head. Jets of fire start up in intervals, and I jump and contort my body, swiftly moving around the streams of fire.

"Fuck me, someone remind me why we signed up for this again?" Nate says from the end of the corridor behind me.

"We didn't," Prince Callan replies.

Heat brushes my face as a stream of fire shoots out in front of me, and I flick my head back, narrowly avoiding the flames. *Twenty. Twenty-One. Twenty-Two.* The fire stops, and I shoot forward four more steps before dropping to the floor and avoiding three jets of fire that surround me. *Twenty-Nine. Thirty. Thirty-One.* I keep counting.

By the time I make it to the end of the corridor, sections of my clothes are singed, and I have burn marks on my arms, but I'm whole. I plant my feet on the stone before the double doors at the end, and I blow out a breath.

"Well, that wasn't so bad," I say to Shade.

"Speak for yourself," she grumbles, popping her head out from where she'd burrowed into my bodice and is squeezed between my breasts. *"If anyone asks, tell them I flew through there."*

"Will do," I grin as I pull down the lever and the jets of fire stop. The guys all come across, and Dante leans close and whispers in my ear, *"Well done, princess."* I shiver as his warm breath touches my skin, and I turn to the doors leading away from the corridor of fire.

Dante grabs the steel knobs.

"This is the last room," I say. "Beyond these doors is the great hall. It's where the royals usually meet to carry out sensitive discussions involving the different realms."

"And it's where we'll find the gateway," Prince Callan adds, and I'm reminded that he's probably attended some of the meetings held here as well.

"Everyone ready?" Dante asks.

I nod. If I'm right, this will also be where we'll encounter the last trial the king has left for us. *And then we can go home.*

"Let's get this over with," Alaric growls, his body rigid.

Dante pushes the doors open, but before he can take a step, I fist the back of his shirt, stopping him from moving forward. His eyes widen as he pulls his boot back and away from the swirling shadows that cover the floor. Well, they don't cover the floor, because there *is* no floor. Instead of the white tile flooring that's usually in this room, black shadows writhe and curl around one another like snakes.

Nate's expression slackens. "What the fuck is that?"

I grimace. "That would be a gateway to the shadow realm."

"The shadow realm?" Prince Callan frowns. "But that's forbidden."

"Feel free to tell that to the demon king when you see him," I say, indicating with my hand to a space on the opposite end of the room where a smaller gateway is burning in a section of the wall. Unlike the blanket of shadows that's an opening to the shadow realm, this gateway burns with red fire. I'm guessing the king has his best guards on the other side of that portal awaiting our return.

"But how?" Prince Callan questions, his gaze fixated on the shadows.

I can't imagine what deal Dad's made with Queen Krosia, the ruler of the shadow realm, for her to open such a large gateway here, and I shudder as I think of the last time I'd been in her realm. "Let's just say Dad has connections," I reply.

There's a series of obstacles around the room that can be used to travel across the open floor toward the portal to Seral. There are levitating stones, thick steel beams, and even some suspended netting. It wouldn't be impossible to jump from obstacle to obstacle, but it'd be difficult.

"I'm guessin' going back aint an option?" Nate says as he assesses the room in front of us.

"Not if you want to get out of Perstalia," I answer. "Knowing the king, this is our only way out of this."

"What about the other alphas?" Prince Callan asks, and I wonder if he's thinking about Saphis and the other archangels.

"This isn't meant for them," I reply, my gaze flicking to the last levitating stone before the gateway to Seral where a familiar-looking dagger is resting on its side. *Unbelievable.* It's the same dagger I retrieved from the shadow realm for the king not too long ago. "This has been left here for me and my mates. It's the final test. Once it's complete and we're back in Seral, we can organize the retrieval of everyone else."

Prince Callan stretches out his wings. "Shall we fly this time?"

I peer at Nate and Alaric, and this time neither of them protest at the idea of being carried.

"Flying would be the fastest way across," I say, "but this will only work if we can keep the shadows out of our minds. The shadow creatures that guard the gateways of the shadow realm feed on fear, and once they're in your head, they'll try to break you. I hope your hesitancy to let us carry you before was because of pride and not fear, because if you let the creatures drag you to the shadow realm you might not ever make it out."

Dante stares down at the curl of shadow reaching for his ankle. "Then I think we'd best keep our wits about us," he comments with a tight smile.

"Blake, I don't like this," Shade whispers, her voice wobbling.

"We'll be fine, just stick close to me," I reassure her. *"We'll be back in Seral before you know it."*

Nate blows out a breath.

"All right, Prince Callan, if you take Dante," I say, "I'll take Nate. Then I'll come back for Alaric." With my strength power, I could probably carry two of my mates at the same time, but I don't want to risk accidentally dropping one of them.

"Let me come back for the assassin," Prince Callan says, but I shake my head.

"I don't trust you not to drop him," I say.

I can tell Prince Callan wants to protest further, but he only nods in resignation like him dropping the assassin was entirely possible.

"Huh. Guess the prince finally hates someone more than me," Nate comments with a grin.

Prince Callan scowls at the shifter. "I wouldn't go that far, Nine Lives."

I lift my hands. "Okay, everyone needs to calm down if we're going to get through this in one piece."

"I'll wait here with the giant," Shade says, landing on the ground near Alaric's feet.

I purse my lips. I know she's just trying to delay

her trip across, and I'd rather her fly with me now, but I don't push it.

Dante gives me a devilish grin. "Time to get out of here," he says, and he grabs onto Prince Callan who's still scowling. The archangel doesn't look impressed, but he wraps his arms around the demon.

Nate smiles at me. "Shall we, gorgeous?"

Before I can respond, he jumps into my arms, and I catch him, cradling him like a baby. *Well, this isn't weird at all.*

"Mmmm, you smell so good," Nate comments as he tucks his head against my neck, nuzzling in close.

I bite my bottom lip, fighting against the need that races through my body. "Okay, here we go," I say to Prince Callan, and I stretch out my wings and lead the way.

~ Alaric ~

I glower at the shifter as he cozies up to the demon princess, taking advantage of the situation as she carries him across. Below them, the shadows swirl like they've been upset by a gust of wind as they pass, but all of them make it to the levitating platform on the other side of the room without incident. When they set down, Nate climbs from the princess's arms, and she picks up a jeweled dagger that's been left at their feet and tucks it into her belt. She whispers something to the others, and then she's heading back my way.

Her bird companion bounces around nervously near my feet.

"Breathe, little one," I tell her. "There are times when even the weakest must display acts of bravery."

The crow cocks her head and glares at me, but I turn my attention to the demon princess who draws close.

"Great pep talk," Princess Blake says sarcastically as she sets down beside me.

I frown, surprised by her comment. "Did I say something offensive?"

The crow is shaking her head now, and I don't understand what's happening. Princess Blake seems to take pity on me, because she answers. "It's best not to call a girl weak, especially when she's about to fly across a gateway to the shadow realm."

"But she is weak. I could easily crush her in my fist if I wanted," I reply. "I was merely trying to comfort her."

The crow ruffles her feathers showing her displeasure, and the princess lets out an exasperated sigh. "Just grab on, big guy. Let's get this over with."

I remain bewildered, but I move to the she-demon's side, wrapping my arms around her. She feels small and fragile in my arms, but she holds onto me and flaps her wings steadily, easily lifting us into the air.

"Try not to move too much," she tells me. "Or you might upset my balance."

I take her request seriously and keep still, even as my cock hardens, her intoxicating scent of cinnamon and honey filling my nose. She sucks in a sharp breath like she's just as affected by our close proximity as I am, and the hint of a smile pulls at my lips.

Her little feathered friend flies beside us as the princess starts to carry us across, and I force myself to clear any negative thoughts from my mind. The shadows whisper below me, calling my name, but I think of the snowy mountains in Rostof, where I have a small cabin that's hidden away from the world. I don't get there often, but when I do, I relax by the fire, listening to the crackling flames and sinking into my favorite armchair. When I'm in the cabin, I can block out all the noise of the past. And of the present. I'm thinking of the snowy caps I can usually see through the windows of the cabin, and the rainbow of colors that fill the sky for months of the year, when the princess's panicked voice jolts me from my thoughts, her grip tightening on me.

"Shade, what are you doing?" she hisses.

I blink, watching as the little bird flies lower, leaving our side and descending toward the shadows below which swirl, coiling around each other like vipers waiting to attack.

"Shade!" Princess Blake calls out again, but the crow continues downward.

"Fuck! They have her," Princess Blake curses, and then we're dropping lower as well.

"If the shadows have penetrated her mind, there's no saving her," I say bluntly, and the princess glares at me.

Despite the anger in her eyes, I see the fear there. The desperate, chilling fear for her friend. "Screw that," she says, her lips set into a hard line. And then she drops me.

I land on a platform not far from the archangel prince and the others, and Princess Blake moves faster without my added weight, flapping her wings harder as she rushes toward her friend.

"Blake!" I hear Dante cry out, but she ignores him, flying headfirst toward the shadows, her arms outstretched.

"Snap out of it!" she yells at her friend, but the bird only flies steadily downward, her beady black eyes unfocused.

I clench my jaw, and I don't think as I start to leap between obstacles, moving closer to the pair of them.

The crow is almost at the shadows, and they writhe beneath her like they're desperate for a taste of her.

Closer, the bird flies toward them.

The black shadows form clawed hands, dozens of them reaching out and swiping at the air, but just as they're about to take her, just as the shadowy fingers prepare to drag her into the shadow realm, Princess Blake grabs hold of her friend's little body, and the she-demon swoops upward with the crow in her grasp.

I don't want to acknowledge the relief that goes through me.

The princess flies higher again, but the layer of shadows ripples below, angry whispers exploding into the air around us.

"Save me," my twin brother, West's, voice carries on the air, but I ignore it, even as my heart clenches. It's not him, and I won't let the shadows lead me to a pointless death.

"Get to the gateway!" Princess Blake shouts as some of the shadows form up beneath us, and I begin making my way back in the direction of the portal to Seral.

The platform I'm on shakes, and I adjust my stance, stopping myself from losing my balance and tipping over the edge. Peering down, I watch as a creature emerges from below. The dragon is the size of a horse, made of shadow with hollow eyes and smoky wings that carry it swiftly through the air. It soars past me, and the other males try to pierce the creature with their swords as it flies close to their platform. "Your weapons will be of no use," I shout, knowing full well that an ordinary blade can't harm a shadow creature.

Princess Blake flaps her wings harder as the dragon curves toward her. "Just get to the gateway!" she yells again, but none of us move toward the portal. The crow is limp in the princess's hold, and the shadow dragon roars as it draws closer to her, an unnatural cry coming from between its smoky lips.

Prince Callan stretches out his hands, and a gust of wind rushes around the room, but it doesn't do anything to the shadow creature. Nate roars, now in his beast form, but more shadow creatures are forming below us, disturbed from their slumber, and he leaps out of the way as a second dragon flies past me and lunges toward him. Dante dodges to the side and sticks out his sword, but it passes through the dragon's belly without causing harm.

The dragon pivots, setting its sights on me, and I jump to a section of netting further to the side of the ballroom and swiftly climb up it. The beast follows, shadowy talons curling around the steel bands that hold the netting together.

"The only thing that can harm these creatures is a shadow blade," I yell, watching the dragon, even as more shadow creatures begin forming beneath us.

"A what?" Princess Blake calls out, dodging the closing jaws of the dragon behind her.

"It's an ancient blade," I shout, "that was forged within the shadow realm itself. But I heard it was stolen from Queen Krosia some time ago."

For a moment, she doesn't answer, and I leap to another platform.

"Ah crap, no wonder Dad gave me that look when I brought him the dagger from the shadow realm. It was never bloody his," Princess Blake finally rambles, and I have no idea what she's going on about. She pulls the jeweled blade from her belt, the dagger that had been left on the platform near the gateway to Seral.

In a swift movement, the princess pivots in the air, dropping low and lifting the dagger as the shadow dragon passes overhead. The blade plunges into the shadow dragon's belly, and the beast cries out as its flesh solidifies just long enough for the blade to cut a long wound along the length of its torso. And then the creature is falling back toward its brethren.

The second dragon jumps from the netting and flaps its wings, its jaws outstretched toward me, but Princess Blake yells out and I lift my hand in time to catch the dagger she's tossed my way. I bury the blade between the dragon's eyes, and the beast thrashes and cries as it rears back and falls, taking the dagger with it.

Not wasting time, I leap to my feet, and the five of us make our way back to the last platform before the portal to Seral.

Princess Blake peers below. "What's the bet Dad promised Queen Krosia she'd get her blade back," she grumbles. "Least I've helped him keep his word." Her chest heaves as she stares at us. "Okay, now will you guys finally listen and get in the damn portal?"

Dante grins. "Ladies first."

She lets out a pained noise. "We'll go together. Okay?"

There's nodding, and she lets out a long breath. "Good."

The moment I step into the gateway behind the

others, I know something is wrong. The swirling red around us starts to change, the liquid energy lightening in color until silver streams blur past us. I open my mouth to shout a warning, but no sound comes out as we're propelled forward. The blinding streams of silver swirl in a frenetic circular motion around us, and I reach for the blades at my hips.

Before I can draw a weapon, we're through the portal, emerging on the other side, and I lash out when someone tries to grab me. There's a shout as my fist connects with soft flesh, but then something is pushed over my face, and I scent a sickening, herby smell before I black out.

CHAPTER

TWENTY-FIVE

~ Princess Blake ~

I wake to the feel of a silk pillow beneath my head, and there's a brief moment when I think I'm back in Seral. That is, until the scent of roses reaches my nose, the flowery perfume so strong it makes me want to gag. Bolting upright, I grab for my weapons, but my fingers slide against smooth velvet, and my heart thunders when I realize my blades are gone. I blink rapidly in the bright light, glaring down at the white velvet gown fitted to my body with a long slit that reaches up my left thigh. A metal cuff is fastened to my right ankle, chaining me to the bed, but when I try to use my strength to kick my leg free, all I manage to do is pull the chain so tight the cuff pinches my skin. Pain zaps up my ankle making my teeth chatter, and I curse. Whatever it's made of the cuff isn't ordinary metal. Trying to keep my cool, I take a deep breath as the pain passes, and I assess where I am. The four-poster bed I'm on is covered with gauzy white material that drapes down and there's a beautifully carved wooden dresser on my right. Along the walls, a detailed painting of a mountain shrouded by clouds is depicted to my left, and I stare in confusion at the sparkling white crystals embedded into the picture.

Squawking sounds from across the room, and I spot Shade standing on a silver perch inside a large cage that hangs from the ceiling. I blink, staring back at my hands as I remember how I'd been holding her when we'd emerged from the portal, but then I look to the cage again. Shade's feathers are ruffled like she's been roughly handled, and she watches me with panicked black eyes. I open my mind, trying to use my magic to communicate with her, to soothe her, but I can't find her voice, like somehow, we've been disconnected. *Like fuck if anyone puts my girl in a cage.* I reach down and use my hands to try and pry away the cuff on my ankle again, but another intense wave of pain shoots through me, and I last a few seconds before snarling and releasing the metal. Shade squawks frantically, and I pivot to where she's indicating with her beak to a door on the opposite side of the room.

Crap. I scan around, looking for anything that I can use as a weapon, but there's only silk pillows and a large downy blanket. I'm not too worried about that fact. I don't need weapons to be deadly, it just would have made this whole thing a lot easier.

The moment the door opens, I tense, mentally preparing myself to fight, but my jaw slackens as a single figure strides through the doorway.

The male is handsome with long flowing dark hair that reaches his waist, and white eyes that shine like crystals, but it's not his eyes that I'm gaping at. From the waist down, his body has the form of a sleek black stallion, with four strong legs and wide black hooves. Even more strange, are the feathery onyx wings folded behind his back.

"I see you're awake," the stranger says with a smile, his hooves clopping on the floor as he walks into the room. His voice is musical and alluring, but my skin prickles, my instincts telling me this is all wrong.

"Who are you?" I bite out, not bothering with niceties, because if this guy was friendly I wouldn't be chained to a bed right now.

The male's crystal eyes sparkle as he stops a short distance away. Instead of answering my question, he goes on to say, "I've been very patient with your kind, allowing you to visit my city for some time now, but when such a large number of you invaded the city, well, I thought I was going to have to decree a battle order. That is, until I realized the strange males were all there because of some kind of game, and they were trying to find a female.

You see, I then had to discover who you were for myself."

My heart starts pounding an erratic beat in my ears. "Wait. You were watching us?" I think of all the times in Perstalia that I felt as if someone was out there observing me. I'd thought it must have been because Alaric had been stalking me, but now, I think of the three black feathers I found, feathers that I thought were my own. Glossy black feathers that are the same as the ones this male has, and I realize my mistake.

The male strolls around the room as he speaks, and I can't stop staring at his massive hooves. "Well, you weren't hard to find, and now I understand what all the fuss was about," he replies.

"I don't know what you want from me. Our intention was never to invade. We were sent here," I try to explain, but he goes on.

"Luckily for you I was able to step in, and you no longer have to worry about those unsavory males who have been hunting you."

Panic makes my heart squeeze. *The guys.* "What have you done with them?" I ask, my breathing becoming shallow.

"They're alive for now, but like I said, you won't have to worry about them any longer. From what I've seen, you should be thanking me."

Shade starts squawking, and he walks over to her cage and smirks like he enjoys seeing her like that. "You shouldn't give your pet so much freedom, you know," he comments. "I, more than anyone, know the importance of protecting those we love."

I want to point out that sticking Shade in a cage isn't protecting her, but I'm still focused on my guys. Shade might be locked away, but at least I know where she is. Even if she is going to be pissed when she gets free. "Tell me where my mates are," I say, my hands curling into fists.

He smiles cruelly. "Let's just say they're being put to good use."

I grind my teeth and try to calm my panic by reminding myself that at least the guys are still alive. For now, anyway. I'll find a way to free them, but first, I need to get myself out of this mess. "I don't understand any of this," I say, backing up to some of the previous information he revealed. "You said that Perstalia is *your* city? You still haven't told me who you are."

His appreciative gaze slides up my body before his gaze meets mine. "Why I'm King Celzar, proud ruler of Perstalia, or as we like to call our new home, The Haven. And you, my beloved, are to become my bride."

WANT MORE?

Thank you for reading Deranged Demons! The story continues in book 2: Ruthless Monsters. If you enjoyed the first part of Princess Blake's story, it would mean the world to me if you could leave a review on Amazon or Goodreads. Honest reviews are important for indie authors because they help readers discover our books. Thank you!

If you'd like to read more about this world, sign up to Mia Hartson's mailing list via her website www.miahartson.com/derangeddemonssignup and you'll receive a free copy of the (100-page) novella, *Delicious Demons*, which is a side story to the Game of Psychos series, and is set in Seral City. The story follows the truth-teller, Scarlett, and details how she finds her fated mates.

Also by Mia Hartson

HER CURSED PROTECTORS

Shadow Shifter (prequel)

The Blood of Monsters

The Cries of Monsters

The Curse of Monsters

The Wars of Monsters

Blurb for The Blood of Monsters:

Every decade, twelve young women from my island are gifted to the monsters.

This year, I'm in the line-up. But unlike the others, I want to be taken. Correction, I *need* to be taken—for my sister's sake. It's my fault she was chosen during the last offering, and I have to find out if she's alive.

I thought I was ready, but nothing could have prepared me for the four monsters who claim me. A vampire, wolf shifter, demon, and siren. They're terrifying, powerful, and infuriatingly arrogant...and now these alphas are fixated on me.

Turns out, finding my sister won't be as easy as I'd hoped. Now that I'm in their world, the monsters think I'll become one of them. I'm in their monster trials, and they're going to play with me until I turn.

These assholes think it'll be easy to break me, but they picked the wrong girl. Because I'm already a monster. They just don't know it yet.

*This is a fun reverse harem fantasy novel for audiences aged 18 years and older. **Language warning **Slow burn romance **Multiple POV*

ABOUT THE AUTHOR

Mia Hartson is a fantasy and paranormal romance author who enjoys writing about strong heroines who aren't afraid to get their hands dirty (or bloody), and hunky, misunderstood heroes who would do anything to protect their girl.

Mia lives in Adelaide with her husband, two girls, and her fur baby. When she's not writing, she's devouring another book, binging the latest fantasy TV series, or going on adventures with her family.

For more information about Mia Hartson, her books, and upcoming releases visit:

Website: www.miahartson.com
Facebook page:
www.facebook.com/AuthorMiaHartson
Facebook reader group (Mia's Mischievious Monsters):
www.facebook.com/groups/miahartsonsmischievousmonsters
Goodreads: www.goodreads.com/author/show/22415741.Mia_Hartson

Instagram: www.miahartson.com/authormiahartson
Bookbub: www.bookbub.com/authors/mia-hartson
TikTok: www.tiktok.com/@miahartsonauthor